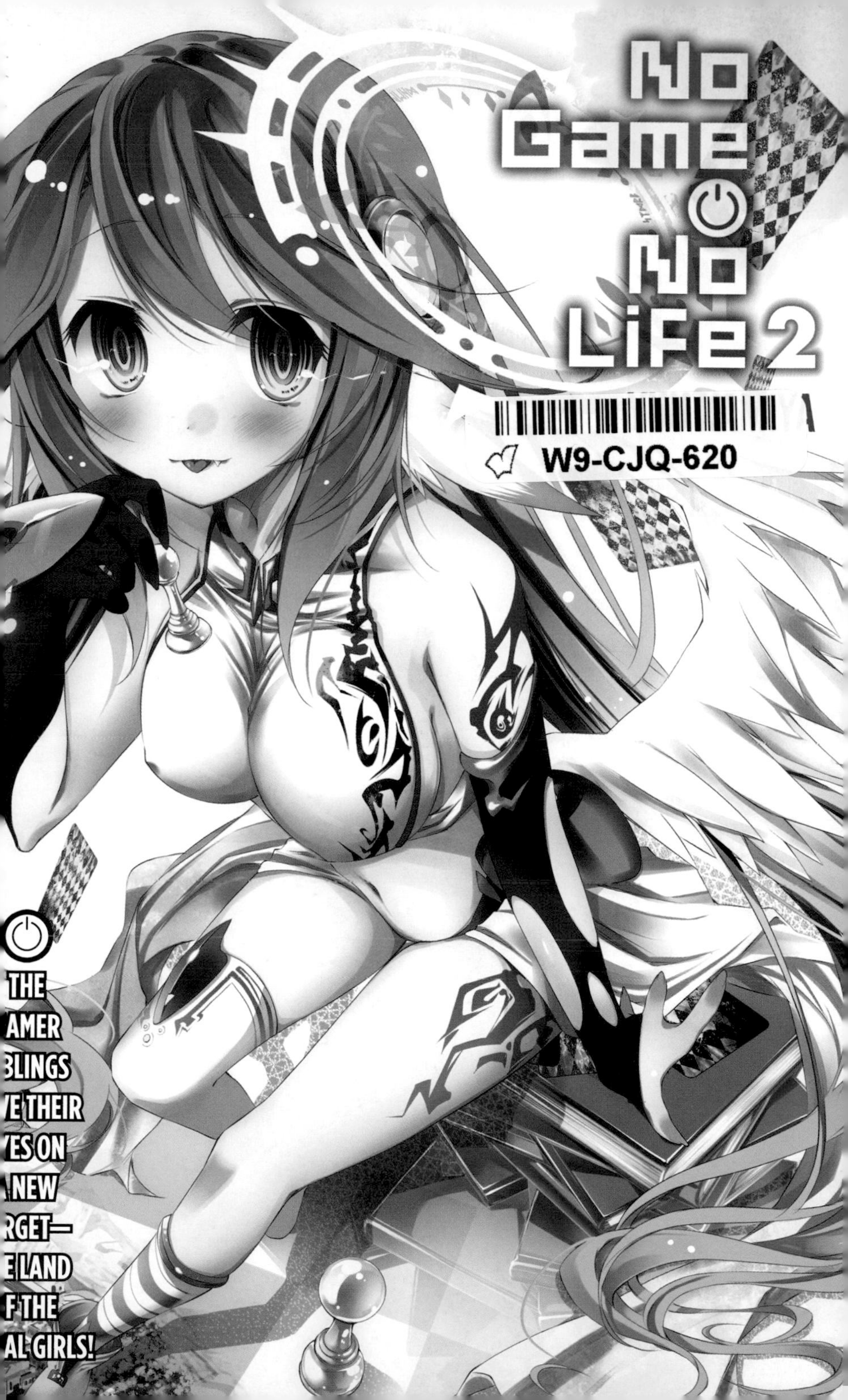
No Game No Life 2
THE
AMER
BLINGS
VE THEIR
YES ON
NEW
RGET—
E LAND
F THE
AL GIRLS!
W9-CJQ-620

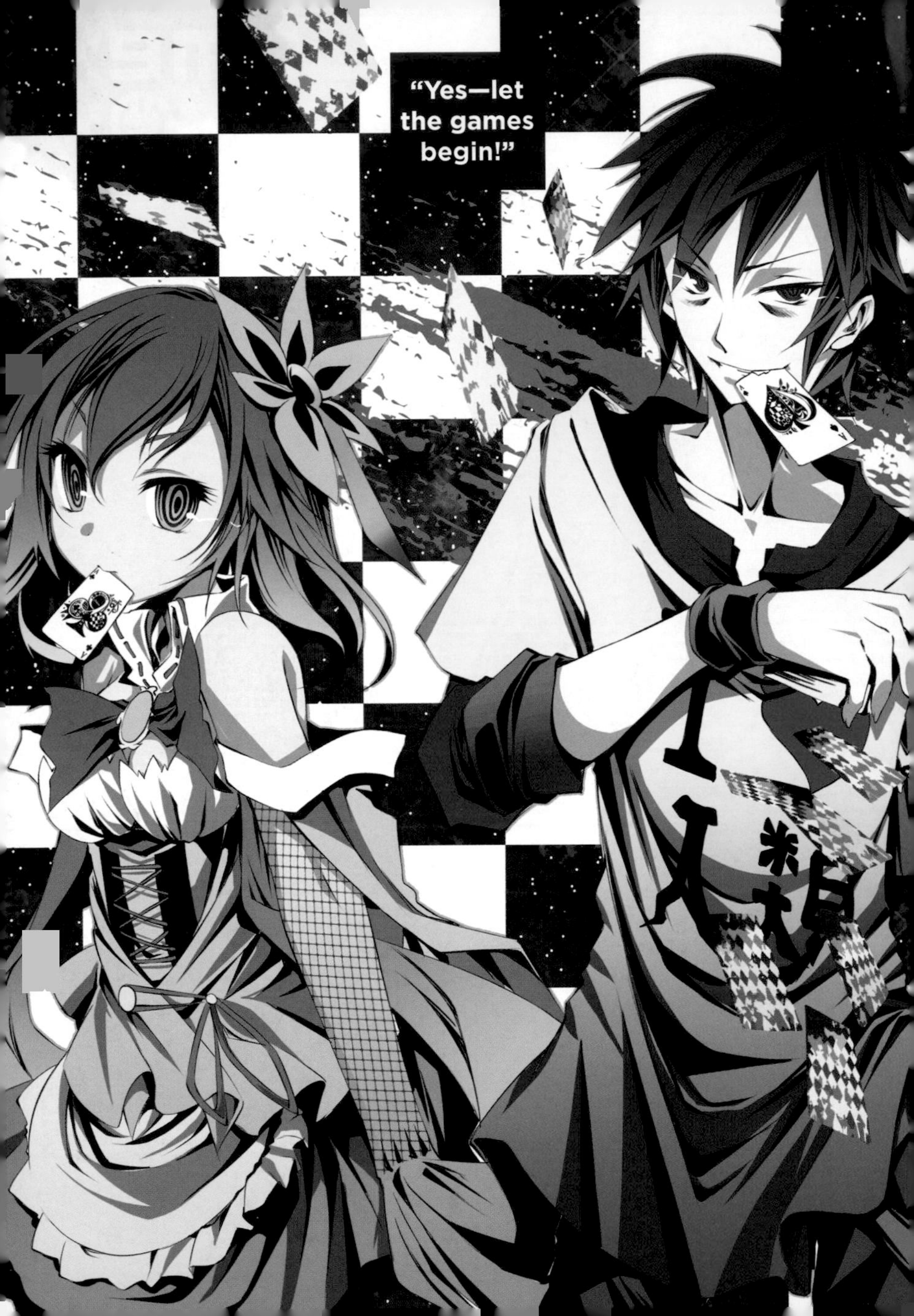
"Yes—let the games begin!"

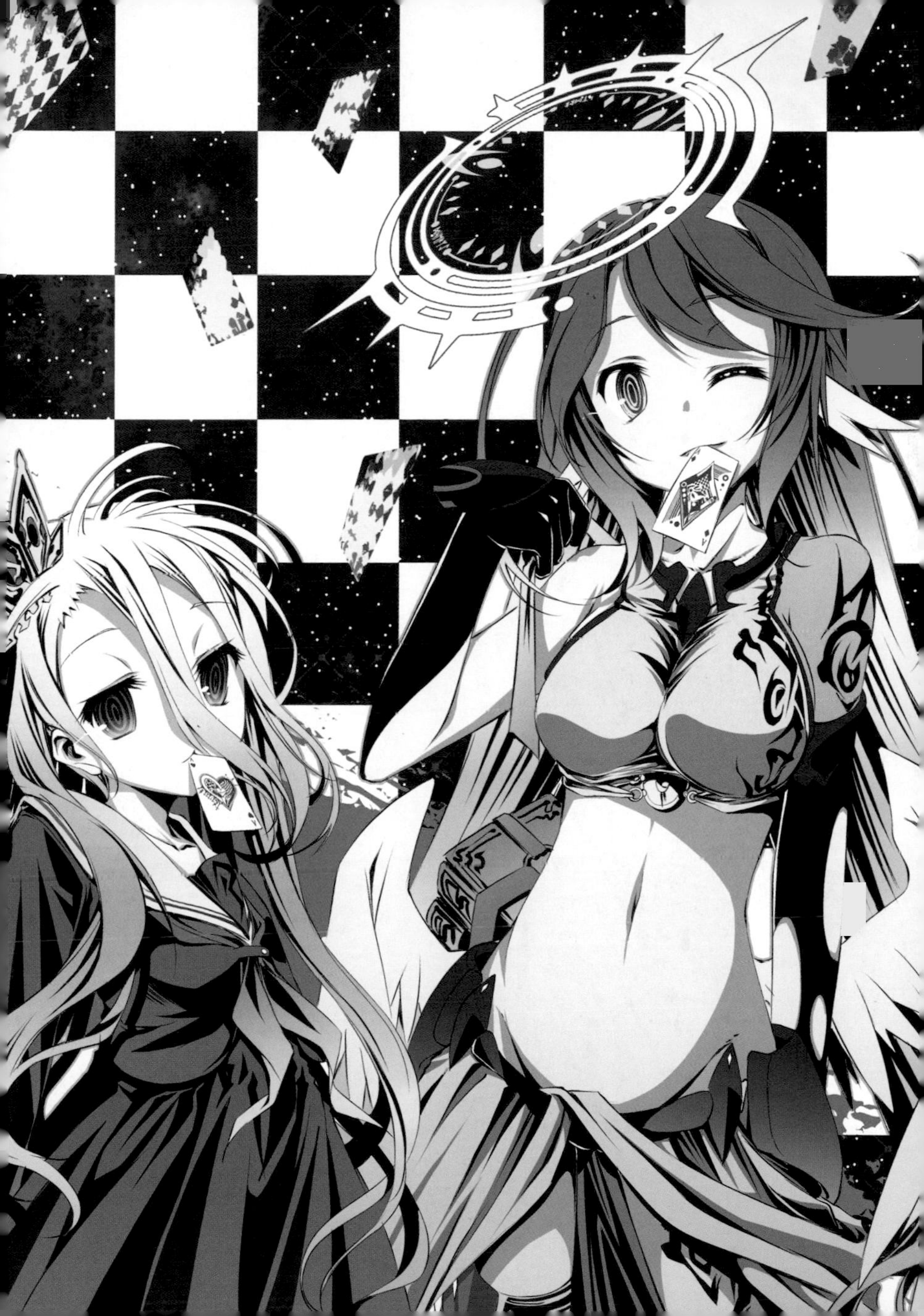

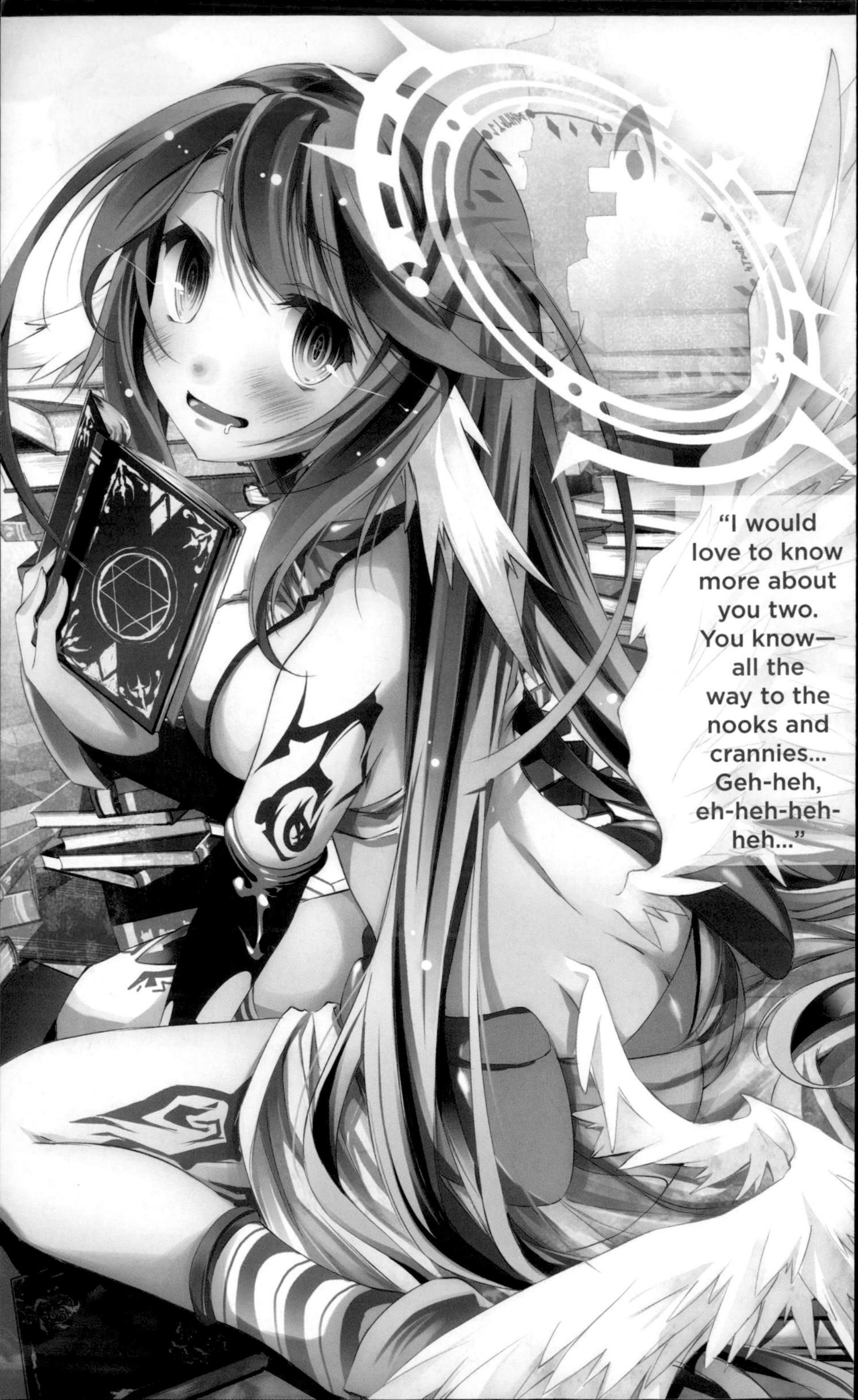
"I would
love to know
more about
you two.
You know—
all the
way to the
nooks and
crannies...
Geh-heh,
eh-heh-heh-
heh..."

"Before the Ten Covenants, we liked to collect *heads*."

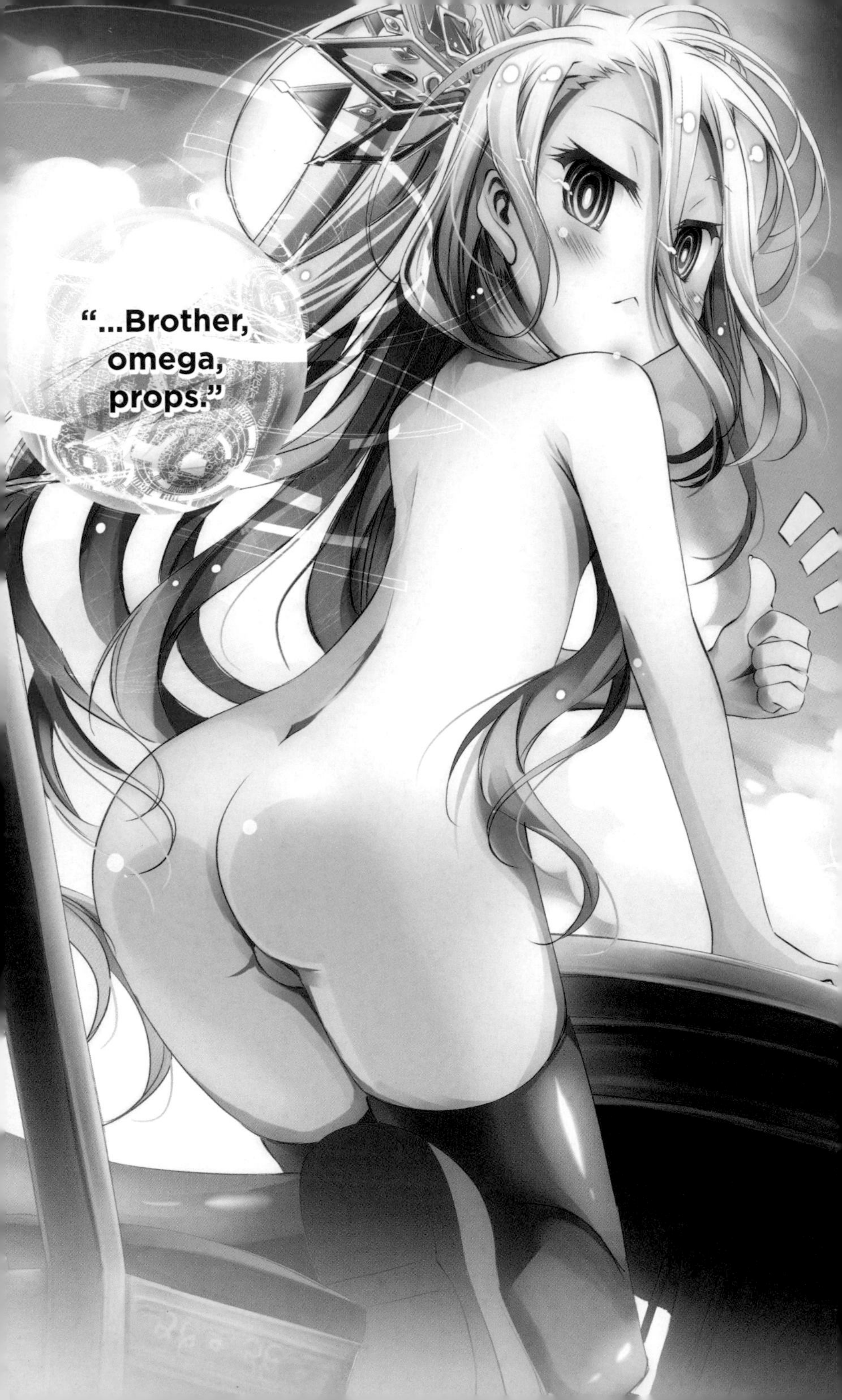
"...Brother,
omega,
props."

"There can be no doubt that this is **appropriate for all ages**! Healthy and **wholesome**! Tastefully **erotic**! But not obscene! For this is what I shall henceforth name: the **Great Wholesomeness Space**!"

Eeplaaaaaaaaaaaaah!

CONTENTS

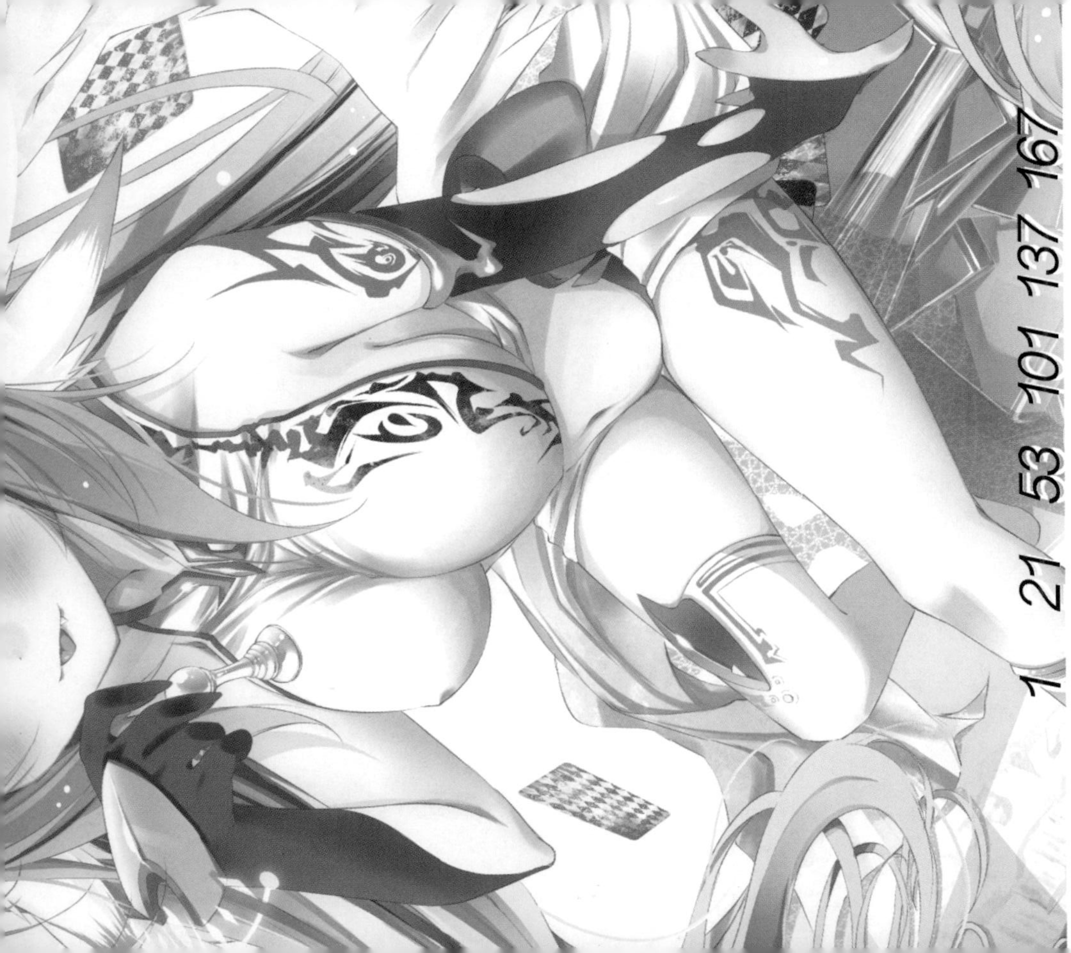

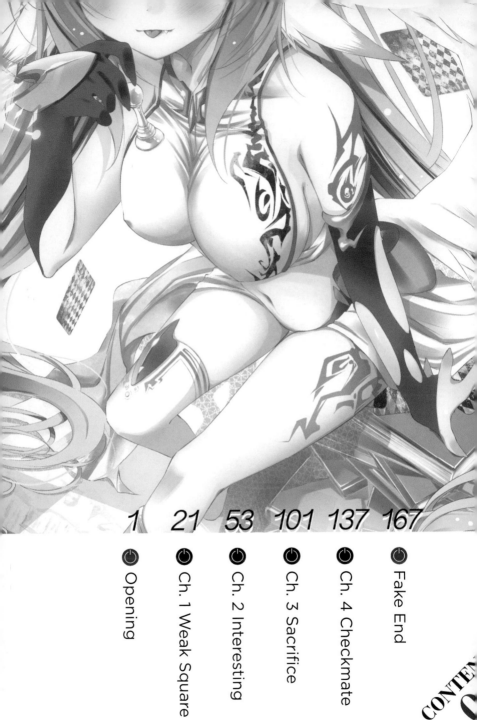

No Game No Life

YUU KAMIYA

2

YEN ON
NEW YORK

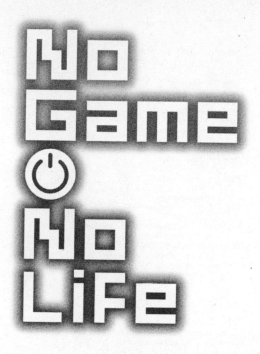

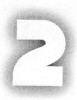

NO GAME NO LIFE, Volume 2
YUU KAMIYA

Translation by Daniel Komen

NO GAME NO LIFE
©YUU KAMIYA 2012
First published in 2012
by KADOKAWA
CORPORATION, Tokyo.
English translation rights reserved
by Yen Press, LLC
under the license from KADOKAWA
CORPORATION, Tokyo,
through Tuttle-Mori Agency,
Inc., Tokyo.

English translation © 2015 by
Yen Press, LLC

Yen On
1290 Avenue of the Americas
New York, NY 10104
www.yenpress.com

Yen On is an imprint of Yen Press,
LLC.
The Yen On name and logo are
trademarks of Yen Press, LLC.

The publisher is not responsible for
websites (or their content) that are
not owned by the publisher.

First Yen On Edition: July 2015

ISBN: 978-0-316-38517-6

10 9 8 7 6

LSC-C

Printed in the
United States of America

⏻ OPENING

You're playing an RPG, and you hit a door you can't open. Isn't this what you think? *If I can use magic, why can't I just bust this door the hell open?* But you can't. Why not? Because those are the *rules*.

—Games and real life are different. People like to say this as if you can't tell the difference. But have they thought about *how* they're different? They're probably just thinking in terms of *is it real or not?* Now, as much fun as it might be to debate whether sports are reality or a game, we won't go there. What I want to talk about is a more fundamental difference between games and reality: *absolute rules*.

If we look at the previous example *realistically*, ignoring rules, you don't need to worry about a door. You can just break it and continue. When the fate of the world is at stake, who needs to look for the key? If all you need is a key to claim whatever's inside as your own, then it seems like even if you just smashed the chest open, you're hardly going to get sued for destruction of property. Looking at it another way, if the door is so strong that you can't even break it with magic capable of defeating the Devil, couldn't you just break through the wall instead? Heck, you could even grab that insanely tough door and use it as a shield while fighting the Devil. Same for the legendary sword in the stone: You don't have to pull the sword out—just break the stone. But they don't do that. Why not?

Because then it would be boring.

That's right: Rules are there to make the process of reaching the end fun. In *shogi*, to capture the king; in soccer, to score more goals; in an RPG, to defeat the final boss. There's nothing cool about reaching the end without following the rules. Thus, the rules of games have a *shared absoluteness.*

—Do you see it yet? In reality—there is no ending. Victory isn't secured when certain conditions are fulfilled, and beating someone doesn't bring peace. Lovers never live happily ever after. For better or for worse, for richer, for poorer, every single relationship reaches a *dead end.* Therefore, people set their own endings *using their own arbitrary interpretation*, and they create their own arbitrary rules to go along with them. *If I make more money, I win. If I have more fun, I win.* Just thinking in terms of winning in the first place makes you a loser...

Let's try a little thought experiment. Imagine you're playing *shogi*, and all of a sudden, your opponent starts moving pieces around however he wants with no rhyme or reason. And then, without even capturing your king, he looks at you as if to say, *How's that? I won.*
...How did you react? Could it be that you wanted to punch him in the face? But can you think of a game where everyone plays that way? That's right—that's *reality.*

—Games and real life are different? No shit. We have a few words for the people who smugly state the obvious: Don't even try to compare them, n00b.

■■■

Eight twenty-three-inch widescreen monitors. That was the whole of their world.

A little planet, thirteen thousand kilometers in diameter at its equator. A world with its surface covered in a fiber-optic network... Earth. On this planet, the concept of distance had been forgotten. Connecting to the Internet allowed one to transmit thoughts fast enough to go around the world seven times a second. It was possible to connect with someone on the other side of the planet as if they were right by one's side.

—People said the world had expanded boundlessly.
—But they thought the world had *shrunk* suffocatingly.

Everything necessary for life could be delivered with a single click. The discarded boxes robbed the close room of its original breadth. In that enclosed space where the artificial light of their displays blinked upon them—no, rather on the other side of those monitors, the net space built in hexadecimal—that was their whole world.

Cramping the room even further were the countless PCs and consoles. The wiring connecting them and numerous controllers, these things robbed their quarters of even so much as space to walk. Illuminated within this setting were two faces devoid of expression. These belonged to the brother and sister who were presently waging a fierce battle against some unknown players on the other side of the globe. The brother was a young man with black hair and black eyes. The sister was a girl with white hair and red eyes. The contents of the screen were chaotic, while the contents of the room were still. The siblings' headphones even monopolized the sounds of *their true world*. All that could be heard within the room were inorganic, mechanical noises and the clicking of the pair.

* * *

—They thought the world had shrunk. Electronic data networks had enabled the ability to see the other side of the planet without moving. But what that led to was a *data tsunami* that far exceeded the limits of individual cognition. The explosion of data had not created boundless connection, but the opposite. The surplus of information was a poison that made people retreat to their own little worlds which were biased toward what they wanted to hear. Countless little closed communities. Isolated, ever-smaller, shallow individual ideologies. And someplace else, another realm distinct from reality: the boundless universe of games. Their eyes as they peered into the worlds beyond the monitor... Sometimes they concentrated so hard that they fell under the illusion that they were actually in those *other worlds*. That they weren't the dregs of society, bound in this cage the size of sixteen tatami mats. Sometimes they were heroes, standing up to save countries. Sometimes they were heads of the greatest guilds in the land. Sometimes they were mages, sometimes they were elite commandos, sometimes assassins. The common thread was that the world always revolved around them. *Clear victory conditions* were laid out.

The young man let out a sigh. Eight twenty-three-inch widescreen monitors. How long had it been since they had become his whole world?

The two reigned undefeated in all kinds of games. In the little world beyond the monitor, they were practically an urban legend. In the little gaming sphere to which they belonged, they were truly heroes, just like in the games themselves. But whenever they looked away, the scene was the same as ever. Artificial, quiet, cramped. The small, isolated world...of the dregs of society. In these moments, the young man would find himself overwhelmed by a sense of dysphoria, the sensation of *jamais vu*: *Is this really my room?* Taking the thought further, he idly wondered with no basis in reality—*Is this really the world in which I was meant to live?*

* . * *

"Yes, you're right."

A voice responded to his internal monologue. Sora surveyed the same world he and his sister had looked on countless times, but suddenly standing within it—an unfamiliar boy, innocently smiling.

—Wait. Had Sora seen him before? He searched his memory, but before he could speak, the boy went on.

"This isn't where you were meant to live. So..."

And—

"...that's why I've given you a *new life*."

Past and present, fiction and reality. All of Sora's memories clouded. His increasingly hazy consciousness started stripping away the reality of the world. That's when he suddenly realized—*the usual.*

"......*Oh, I see. It's a dream.*"

Then, just like all dreams...it ended. Impossible to pinpoint precisely when, his consciousness returned...

∎∎∎

The Kingdom of Elkia: the capital, Elkia. In this city, now the last bastion of Immanity after losing territory in one failed bid for dominion after another. In a corridor of the Royal Castle, a girl walked unsteadily. Stephanie Dola. A red-haired, blue-eyed noble girl of the finest breeding, granddaughter of the previous king.

—However, the deep fatigue indicated by the dark circles under her eyes and her heavy steps robbed the young lady of her natural refinement. Clutching playing cards with a creepy smile, wobbling her way to the bedchamber of the king, she gave the impression instead of...a ghost.

"Heh, heh-heh-heh... This is the day you get what's coming to you."

As the newly risen sun came to reap her post-all-nighter consciousness, Stephanie—aka Steph—chuckled restlessly.

"—*Sora*, you're awake, aren't you?! It's morning!"

Bam, bam. Her hands preoccupied with cards, Steph kicked the door, rudely addressing the king by his first name. But…

"*Beeep. The party you have dialed is pretending not to be available.*"

"—Huh?"

The voice that answered from inside the room was not the king's. Rather, it was a groggy, monotonous impression of a woman.

"*Please move away from the door immediately and be sure not to barge in.*"

"—Sora, is this some kind of joke?"

"*No, I'm serious, d00d.*"

"For the God's sake! I'm coming in, all right?!"

He was probably just playing a game anyway—wait, scratch that, he definitely was. Spurred on by the irritation of fatigue, as if to kick in the door—no, actually kicking in the door—Steph entered the royal bedchamber to find…

"I'm sorry I'm so sorry I really wasn't joking I honestly just can't right now I didn't mean anything really I'm serious please I'm sorry I'm sorry…"

—The king, crouching on his bed, clutching his head, apologizing profusely. His visible trembling was so pitiful as to elicit tears. However, Steph, having seen something similar before, looked around the room as she spoke. The chamber was littered with so many books there was no place to step. Books and countless games. But what set Steph to muttering was the absence of the thing that *should* have been there but wasn't.

"…Hm? Sora, are you alone?"

"Yes I'm alone so alone no more reason to live probably never should've been born in the first place I'm sorry after you go I'll just be a good boy and hang myself so please—"

"…Brother…? You're making a racket…"

As the king babbled breathlessly, a lethargic voice rose up in complaint. Recognizing it immediately, Steph sighed and murmured:

"So Shiro *is* here. What are you doing?"

"—Huh?"

At this revelation, Sora whipped his head in Shiro's direction. She must have fallen while sleeping. A girl as white as snow, crept up the side of the bed. Sora moved to embrace her in an uproar.

"Ahhhhhhh, I'm sooooo glad! Oh God, my sister! I almost hung myself by mistake thanks to your sloppy sleeping. What do you have to say for yourself?!"

As the brother wept openly, rubbing his cheek against his sister, Shiro. The sister considered him with a cold squint out of sleepiness…though probably not exclusively that.

"…Brother…that's, too much…"

"What?! Are you saying you don't understand your brother's feelings?!"

Sora bolted to his feet and crowed with grand gesture.

"Then tonight! While you're sleeping, I'll put you in the closet! And when you wake up, I won't be—"

"………!…*Hk*…*Ngh*…"

Before he even finished speaking, Shiro already had tears in her eyes, perhaps imagining it.

"See?! Now do you see how I feel?"

"…I'm sor-ry…I'm…sor-ry, for not sleeping better…"

As Shiro wrung out a sincere apology between sobs, Sora stroked her head.

"No, I'm sorry. I went too far. I was a bad brother to make you imagine such a catastrophe."

"…*Hk*… Yeah…"

At this point, the man—who moments before had been shaking like a newborn gazelle and begging forgiveness—turned powerfully, pridefully, back to Steph with a proclamation.

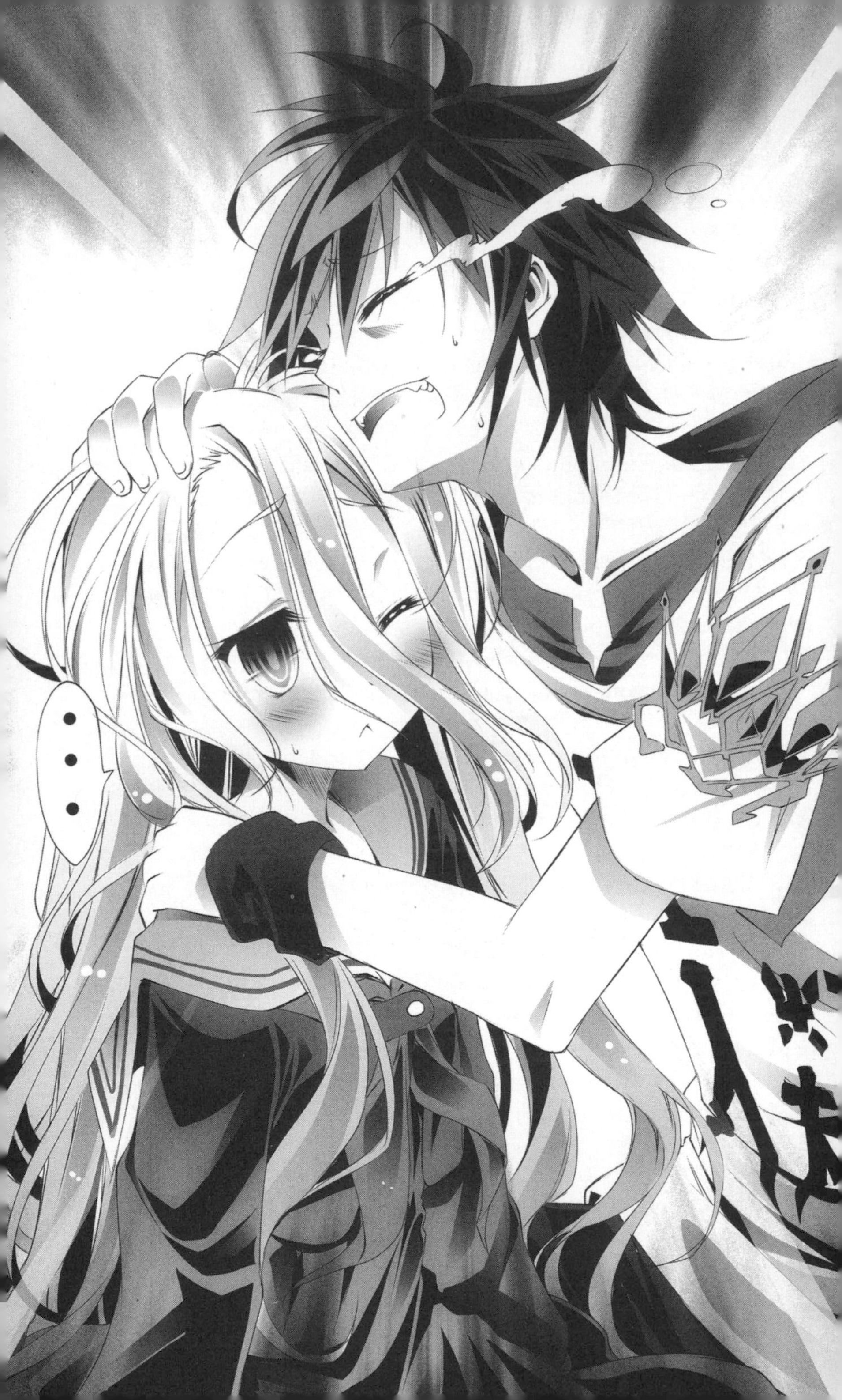
...

"So it must be the bed's fault! Steph, get rid of this bed and lay out a futon!"

"H-hngg?!"

Steph, who had been watching the siblings' antics as if she had already seen it all, raised a queer voice in a panic at the dilemma now facing her.

"Th-th-this is the bed of the royal chamber! Do you know how much history—?"

"Whatever. Sleeping or not, for Shiro to leave my side, it had to be the bed's fault. Maybe it's tilted?"

Shiro instantly nodded in agreement. Steph thought—*How ridiculous.*

"I-I'll have you know that bed is worth enough to feed a whole family!"

"Then sell it and feed a family. It's a good deed. There'll be a happy family."

"…Y-y-y-you…"

As Steph trembled speechlessly at Sora's tyrannical reign, something occurred to the king.

"Oh, right. The stuff in this room belonged to the previous king— your grandfather."

It seemed Steph's reaction had sparked something within Sora. Clapping his hands together, he spoke as if inspired.

"So this is what we'll do: Steph, starting today, *this is your room.*"

"Wha—! …Th-this is the *king's bedchamber!*"

"And I am the king. Anyplace I choose to sleep, be it a doghouse, becomes the *king's bedchamber.*"

Somehow maintaining a straight face, the king spouted off sophistry as if it were breathing to him.

"So get me a room in the building the castle's maids use. For the bed, you should just stick a mattress on the floor, of course."

For a moment, Steph was unable to follow Sora as he declared that a futon would be far, far preferable. After a few seconds, she reacted.

"A-a maid's room…? We're talking about a little shack at the edge of the castle grounds! It's wood, you know?!"

"Mm? Now this I can't overlook. Are you dissing wood?"

Sora cleared his throat with an *ahem* and began.

"It's superior in ventilation, absorbency, insulation, seismic resistance, wind resistance, and everything. Truly a castle as far as a shut-in is concerned. As long as you watch out for fire, there is no architecture that compares to Japanese—"

In the middle of his diatribe, Sora seemed to think of something. Reaching for his *tablet*, which had been on the solar charger by the window...

"Oh, I knew it. I did have a book on Japanese architecture."

"...What?"

"Great, let's build a *house* on the castle grounds!"

"Huh...?"

Leaving Steph behind as she utterly failed to follow him, Sora went on, heated.

"What do you think, Shiro? Our dream, right?! Don't you think that's a great idea?!"

"...Where...would we build it?"

"Heh-heh, I know exactly what your concerns are, my darling little sister!!"

He accentuated his speech with English. As if to say, "You think your brother wouldn't think of that?"...he pointed, *bam*—to the *castle courtyard*.

"Over there, it's closer to the outer ward where the maids stay, so we'd have no problem getting supplies. It's also close to the castle kitchen, so we can shut ourselves in just like always! It's also got a fair amount of greenery and a nice breeze, and very few people pass by! Plus, thanks to the castle wall, there'll be practically *no sunlight at all* in the morning! Can you even imagine a better place than this?!"

Shiro lifted a hand at Sora's boasts.

"...No objections..."

"Great! So, Steph."

"Uh, um, y-yes?"

Steph stood slack-jawed, in awe at these developments.

"Get us some experts on wooden architecture. Yeah, this is probably an unknown style of architecture in this world, so I guess we'll need a few ultra-top-class artisans and twenty or so staff? I guess if we explain how to pick the wood, they can take care of the details."

—By way of a late introduction, these two siblings are Sora and Shiro—the king and queen of Elkia, the last nation of the human race, "Immanity." Who spend days without leaving their room. Who read and play games all day and night while making unreasonable demands.

—This is what you call *tyranny*.

"~~~~~~~*Sora!* Get ready for a *game*!!"

Steph appeared to be out of patience with the tyrants. She clutched her cards in her hands, glaring daggers at Sora as she yelled. For today—she would rain down *divine punishment* upon them.

—But.

"—...Oh?"

At the mere mention of the word "game," Sora's eyes narrowed, all emotion extinguished. Though Steph had seen this instantaneous transformation many times before, it still made her shiver. The pitiful man who just had been shivering had suddenly metamorphosed into a smug, silly big brother. Then with the flip of a switch, the contents of her heart were exposed so that no matter what she did, she'd be in the palm of his hand—his mechanical calmness gave that illusion. With a military boldness, his face became that of a *game master*.

—Considering her response more critically, Steph felt a flash of heat in her face and a skipped beat in her heart as he looked into her eyes. The legacy of the game she had played with him before... The proof that the *tab* from her utter defeat had not been forgotten... This seemed to blunt the resolve with which Steph had arrived. As her ears turned red and her eyes turned away, Sora asked:

"Does this mean you're challenging me to a game under *Aschente*?"

"Uh, why, yes...that's exactly what it means."

"...The Fifth of the Ten Covenants... The party challenged...has the right to determine...the game."

Shiro mumbled out the Covenant she had memorized.

—It was an *absolutely binding Covenant* that the God had set down for this world. An immutable law that could not be defied for any reason.

"Hmmm... And yet...you challenge—me? To a game of *my choosing*?"

—The game had already begun. Steph had readied her counter to Sora's psychological maneuvering.

"Oh, dear me... Could it be you suggest that you, the greatest gamer among humans, will not e-entertain me with a game outside your specialty?"

Though Steph had desperately planned this line out and practiced it. Her voice cracked a bit, and she sounded as if she were reading a script. Sora chuckled and grinned at her smugly.

"I see. So you got a little argument ready ahead of time—what's your wager?"

When playing an absolutely binding game under the Ten Covenants, what to wager was also part of the negotiation.

"Heh-heh-heh... If I win—"

But, as if that question was what she was waiting for, Steph grinned back.

"Sora, you're going to become a decent person!"

Whammo————*!*...Steph's finger leveled at Sora. Then—silence.

"Uh...uh...?"

"Oh, I see how it is." "You got me there." These were the sorts of reactions Steph had been expecting. Instead, Sora shouted with a twinkle in his eye:

"That's—right—if the Ten Covenants are absolutely binding, then they would make that kind of thing possible?!"

"Humgh?!"

As Sora swayed toward Steph with unexpected enthusiasm, Steph averted her face which had erupted in crimson.

"I-I-I mean, you commanded me to fall in love with you...which means—"

—That's right. At the end of their previous game, through some sort of trickery, Sora had demanded that Steph fall in love with him. It was obvious that she had been forced to fall in love with him against her will. Therefore...

"I-I see... I'd totally overlooked that—!!"

This is what it meant to have the scales fall from one's eyes. Sora looked fervently to the heavens but then gasped and shouted again.

"Th-then don't say 'decent person'—make your wager that I *'get a life'*!"

"—Get a...life? What's that supposed to mean?"

"It's an expression. It's pretty much like being a decent person... Come on! Let's bet it, let's play... I'll lose!!"

"Uh, w-well..."

While Steph stood bewildered, unsure how to deal with this manic response, the brakes were suddenly slammed on from an unexpected direction.

"...Brother, you can't...lose to someone other than...me..."

"Wha—?! My—my sister, are you going to life-block your big brother?"

"...Blank can't...lose..."

"*Ngk—!*"

That's right: Sora (Sky) and Shiro (White). When the characters for their names were combined, they formed *Kuuhaku*: "Blank." And " " couldn't lose. It was a promise the two had exchanged back in their *old world*—. In a world without rules, it was an absolute and immutable rule that they had established for themselves. But now Sora looked back in despair as if dropped from heaven to hell.

"That's... But! I mean, there's no way I would actually lose to Steph playing for real!"

"Wha—?!"

The siblings ignored Steph's facial contortion and went on bickering.

"...I don't care..."

"Come—come on, just think! A *life*, a real *life*, with flowers and sparkles and shit! Sh-Shiro, let's do it! You set it as the condition. There's no problem if it's you, right? I'll lose with all I've got! Come on, maybe chess...?"

"...But...I refuse..."

"Aah, God, shit! Steph!!"

"Y-yes?!"

Sora put his hands together in supplication and pleaded with her from his heart.

"I'll stake it on the one-in-a-million—no, *inexpressible-without-imaginary-numbers* chance that you might actually have a game you can beat me at! I'm begging ya, Steph!! Answer my hope, tinier than a quantum!!"

"Heh, heh-heh...hee-hee-hee...hee-hee-hee-hee-hee-hee-hee... Y-you're asking for it, buster!!"

Her face twisted by the rain of verbal abuse, Steph laughed.

"The game is—*blackjack*!"

......

"—...Hhhhh..."

"...Hff..."

As the siblings each heaved their own sighs with their own meanings, Steph wobbled, unable to grasp the implication of either.

"Uh, what? What's that?! I do have a chance at this game?!"

As Sora just sighed again and with Shiro seemingly having lost all interest, Steph yelled:

"I'm the dealer! Sora's the player! This will prevent Sora from cheating, and even if he does, I can catch him and win! Skill has nothing to do with it if it's a *game of pure luck*, right?!"

Sora looking out the window, a single tear glistening on his cheek.

"The character for 'fleeting' is written with 'person' on the left and 'dream' on the right... Well, whatever. Steph, don't lose hope. I'm sure next time you'll blah blah blah."

As Sora messed with his nails and lazily launched into his presumptive victory speech, Steph gnashed her teeth at him.

"H-how dare you...?! J-just you wait! *Aschente!*"

This word was an oath that committed one to an absolutely binding wager under the Ten Covenants—but.

"Yeah, yeah... *Aschente.*"

"Oh, come to think of it, I forgot to say what I would wager..."

"Yeah... Anything's fine, really... *Hff...*"

"Y-you—!"

With Sora's utter conviction of imminent victory goading her, Steph silently reminded herself not to be rattled.

—*That's right, calm down. This is your chance.* Inside, Steph screwed up the corners of her mouth and crowed. A game of pure luck? Like hell. Even though she'd been busy, it went without saying that she'd been practicing a trick all night and was confident she could pull it off. The dealer gets to shuffle the cards. Which meant that if she could line up the cards in the shuffle in a way that *looked* legitimate, she could win. It wasn't as if she'd be slipping in cards. There was no way you could prove it. The Eighth of the Ten Covenants: "If cheating is discovered in a game, it shall be counted as a loss"—which meant *as long as it wasn't discovered, you could cheat*! ("Heh-heh-heh-heh... You'll rue the day you looked down on me!")

—But Steph didn't realize... Such a trick would never be enough to secure her victory over Sora...

■■■

—Beyond the horizon. Chess pieces loomed, massive enough to throw off one's perspective, as if the towering mountains in the distance were merely pedestals for them. Perched atop the king piece, kicking his legs, sat a boy. Whistling merrily, he held a blank book and quill.

"Hmm... It's hard to know where to start."

Apparently thinking about how to start a story he was writing, eventually the boy seemed to think of something and started moving the quill.

"'—Once upon a time, there was a world in which all exercise of armed force was forbidden and all conflicts had to be resolved by games, as an absolute rule...' Yeah. I guess that looks good, more or less?"

Nodding from the top of the piece higher than the heavens, the boy looked far into the distance and muttered:

"...I wonder if it'll start moving soon...*the first piece.*"

The boy's name was Tet. He was the supreme creator of this place—*Disboard*, a world where everything was decided by games. Before the long-ago Great War of the gods put him on the throne of the One True God, he was known as the *god of play*. And now this One True God looked out into the distance, as if projecting his thoughts to a faraway lover.

—*Question: is this a sign of the fall of Immanity?*

This haughty voice suddenly rang out of thin air.

Or: is it a sign that thou wilt at last make thy move?

Seemingly a bit peeved by the intrusion, Tet nevertheless smiled.

"Eavesdropping on me talking to myself? I can't say I think much of your hobby."

The being spying on Tet, the One True God, was able to communicate with him, albeit brokenly. Without a doubt, it was one of the Old Deus, ranked first among the races—and even so, still limited in power. Of course to the One True God, it was obvious who the creature was, though not particularly interesting.

—*Question: Space-time distortion observed before new Immanity monarch determined. Inference that thou wouldst intervene: true, false?*

To this question, Tet merely shot back languidly:

"You guys really are a bore."

As if about to meet his lover again, Tet grinned impatiently.

"I'm not on anyone's side. You don't have to understand. Just go on playing your meaningless games."

And then with a smile that embraced great hope in the midst of great despair:

"*They* are coming. To my doorstep—and you guys can't stop it."

As if (literally) unable to see the disembodied voice resounding around him, he instead turned his gaze to Immanity's last city— Elkia. Though, to the One True God, even hundreds of years must have seemed to pass in the blink of an eye, his eyes were like those of a child standing at the door in anticipation of a trip to an amusement park, unable to wait five minutes for his parents to get ready. Confirming that the presence behind the voice that had rung from the air had vanished with a *ffp*, Tet mumbled:

"Please don't make me wait too long, Blank."

He kicked the edge of the piece he was sitting on with his heels.

"I can hardly stand it anymore. If you make me wait too long—*I'm going to have to visit you, aren't I?*"

Twisting his mouth into an impudent grin, he whispered:

"Oh, that's right. Next—"

Apparently having thought of how to continue his story, Tet twirled his quill.

"'One day, a pair of gamers was invited from another world to a country of Immanity, the lowest-ranking race among the Ixseeds. Coming to the last bastion of beleaguered Immanity—to

Elkia—they defended it from other races and became the king and queen—and that is where everything started'... I like it!"

—The scribbles he wrote, now a story, would soon be an epic passed down among the bards for generations. Penned by the hand of the God himself, foretelling the gods to come. In other words: the prologue to the newest myth—.

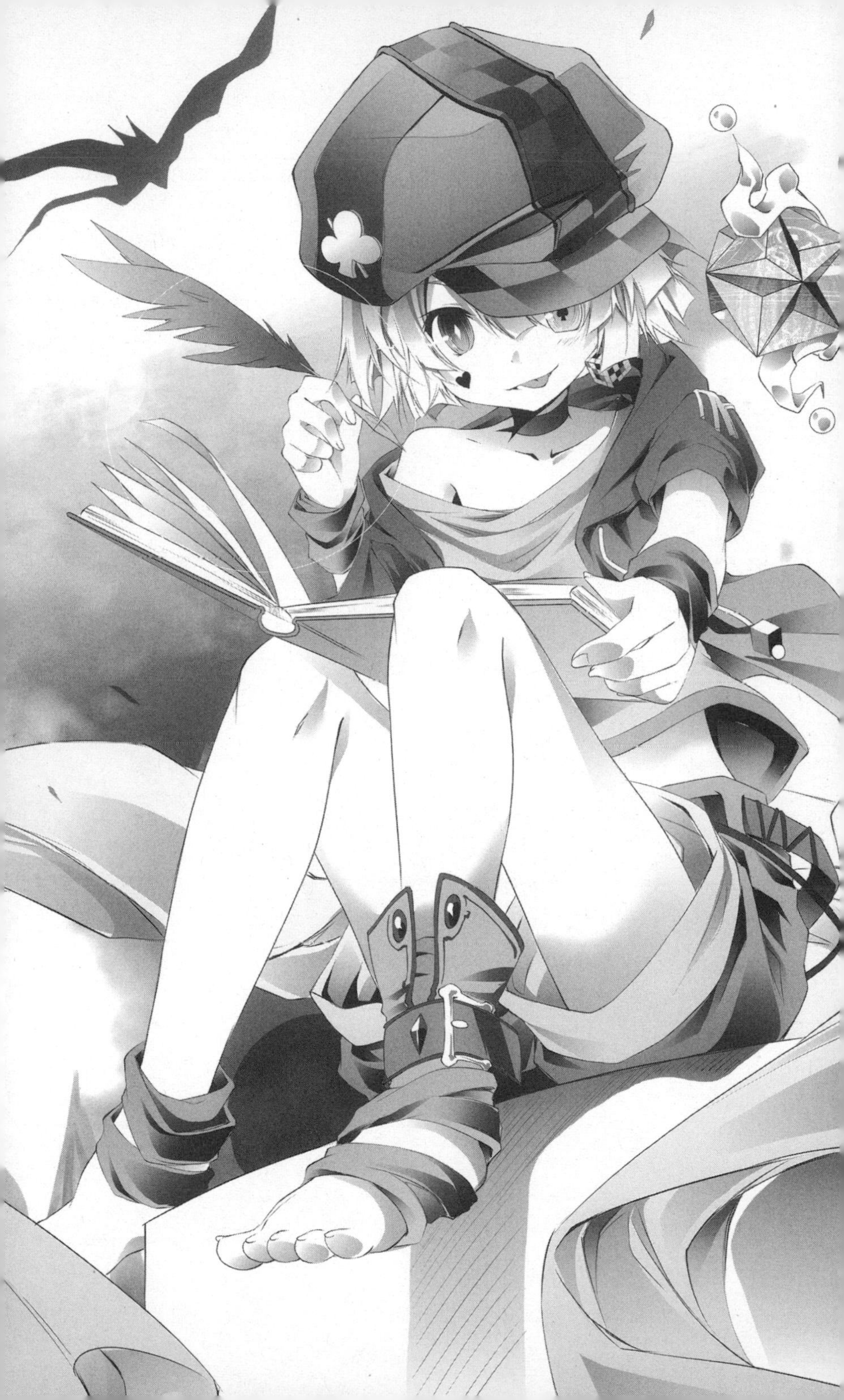

⏻ CHAPTER 1
WEAK SQUARE

The country of Immanity—the Kingdom of Elkia. The capital, Elkia: Block 6, Eastern District. In the guest hall of a resplendent mansion, five people surrounded a table, as several spectators looked on.

One of those at the table was a young man with chaotically sheared black hair and dark circles under his eyes sporting an "I ♥ PPL" T-shirt, jeans, and sneakers. The second was a little girl sitting on his lap—with long, long hair as white as snow, irises red like rubies, eyes deadpan and half-lidded, and wearing a black sailor suit. Around the young man's arm was wrapped the queen's tiara, like an armband. Likewise, the girl used the king's crown to tie her overly long bangs. As it happened, these siblings were collectively the monarch of Elkia, the last nation of Immanity. The brother: Sora. Eighteen, virgin, unpopular, socially incompetent, loser, game vegetable. The sister: Shiro. Eleven, friendless, socially incompetent, shut-in, game vegetable.

......So long, humanity.

* * *

THE END

...Well, that's what anyone would think if that was all they heard. But these two—were not of this world. In their old world, they had set unbeatable records in the rankings for over 280 games. Carving their empty name at the top of all kinds of games without a single loss. And so these gamers, with their unreal skills and mysterious identity, came even to be regarded as the urban legend known as " "—and here they were.

To this world, *Disboard*... Where war had been forbidden by the Ten Covenants since the distant past. Where everything, even nations' borders, was decided by games. At a time when Immanity had been backed into a corner by other races that cheated using magic, which humans could neither use nor even detect. As the last city of Immanity was on the verge of being turned into a puppet state by an Elven spy. To this world, they had come, without magic, without powers. With nothing more than mere human ability, they had earned the crown declaring them the strongest of all humanity, in both name and truth, and had ascended to the throne.

True, they were undeniably failures at life. It was also true that they were inarguably unfit for society. But, in this *one world*—the siblings could very well have been the saviors of Immanity. Of these two in whose hands the hope of Immanity rested, the brother, Sora, cards in hand, spoke!!

"Hey, Steph. Where do babies come from?"

......Perhaps we should say so long after all.

A certain figure watching from the fringes of the table just next to Sora and Shiro, responded with a cold glare.

"...I don't really want to have to explain that to someone upon whose shoulders weighs the fate of Immanity..."

The girl was in her late teens, with red hair, blue eyes, and just the sort of frilly clothing you might expect to see in a fantasy world. Her fashion, her appearance, her manner all suggesting high breeding—Stephanie Dola. Aka Steph. The young miss of a most pedigreed household, once the granddaughter of the king of Elkia, answered:

"—Your Majesty, have you finally lost your mind?" No, that wasn't the right way to put it—she corrected herself. "When I say it like that, it makes it sound as if you were sound of mind to begin with."

"Hey, I'm sound as can be!"

"Asking that question as if it's perfectly rational is exactly what's irrational!"

"Jeez, you just don't get anything! Look, in this world, we have the *Ten Covenants*, right?!"

The *Ten Covenants*. The absolute law of this world, established by the god Tet upon winning the throne of the One True God.

1. In this world, all bodily injury, war, and plunder is forbidden.
2. All conflicts shall be settled by victory and defeat in games.
3. Games shall be played for wagers that each agrees are of equal value.
4. Insofar as it does not conflict with "3," any game or wager is permitted.
5. The party challenged shall have the right to determine the game.
6. Wagers sworn by the Covenants are absolutely binding.
7. For conflicts between groups, an agent plenipotentiary shall be established.
8. If cheating is discovered in a game, it shall be counted as a loss.

9. The above shall be absolute and
    immutable rules, in the name of the God.
10. Let's all have fun together.

"…Yes, and so?"

"I mean, look. Bodily injury is forbidden. So how are you supposed to make babies?"

......

"…May I ask why you are asking this now?"

"I was just bored, and it occurred to me. But isn't this kind of a serious problem?"

Mindful of the gazes around her, Steph whispered at Sora's ear:

"In *your world*, were people born from eggs?"

Yes, it was a secret that Sora and Shiro were from another world.

…Her point being, *don't talk about this in front of all these people.* Steph chastised him with cold, incredulous eyes as usual.

"—H-hey! Don't make fun of me for being a virgin! It's not like I don't know it's, like, the monster in the guy's pocket goes in and out of the girl's secret garden and then the whole world flips, all right?!"

"…Brother, when you, put it like that…it makes you sound, even more…virginal."

"I am a virgin! What do you want me to be if not virginal?!"

The royal gentleman who had never had a girlfriend in his life, childishly rebutted the observations of his eleven-year-old sister perched on his lap.

"A-anyway, when you do that stuff, it causes injury, right?! *At least the first time!!* So with the Ten Covenants, how does Immanity reproduce in this world? That's what I'm asking!"

Steph realized that he might actually be asking a serious question after all. But first—

"…Just let me check: this isn't some fetishy plot to humiliate me publicly, is it?"

"—Um, I think you're the one who's weird for thinking that?"

She could come up with a porn game scenario in a world without porn games. Really, you had to be impressed at that kind of imagination.

"Forget it. I'll just ask someone who knows how to explain things later. Useless."

"Wha— Fine, fine, I'll explain it to you!"

Steph, cleared her throat—*a-ahem.*

"It is clear what constitutes the basis for constituting a violation of rights."

"Hmm. Specifically?"

"Put simply: actions that violate rights *with malice*—are canceled."

...—Wha?

"—Uh...what, are you saying our brains are being censored in real time?"

"Yes, that's quite it."

Okay, while this may have been a fantasy world, you gotta say that's ridiculous.

"Therefore, since the establishment of the Ten Covenants, most laws have become mere relics. After all, any action that is successfully executed has got to be conformant to the Covenants, or else performed by consent or by mistake—"

"*Hhh...* Your God here really can do anything."

"The One True God obviously can do anything, can't he?"

—The right to rebuild the laws of the world on a whim. And now— that itself would be decided by a game in this world, it seemed.

"Hmm... All right, then. So let me ask again, why is making babies okay?"

The one who answered was not Steph, but Shiro, who was on his lap shuffling cards.

"...Consent... 'Transfer'... In other words..."

"Oh, so if you give each other permission, it's not a violation of rights."

Sora, remembering how he was kicked in the back by Shiro before, finally grasped it. If it was Shiro, it was natural to think he might have agreed unconsciously.

∗ ∗ ∗

—With a yawn, Sora mused as he shuffled the cards in front of Shiro:

"Well, that makes sense. I mean, doctors' hands would be tied if you couldn't do anything that wounded another person."

As Sora mumbled again that these sure were well-designed Covenants, Steph commented: "You can see the world is functioning, and the rules are fast."

"That's not how it was back in *our world*..."

...Surprisingly, the world still functioned even without rules, though riddled with contradictions and defects. This world had to have been the same before the Ten Covenants, really.

"...But then that raises another question."

"What is it?"

"Why was I able to fondle your boo— Okay, never mind."

We're in public! If you go any further—Steph's piercing glare was unmistakable, and Sora shut up.

"Anyway, this was a very interesting discussion. Great way to kill time."

"You just explicitly said it was only to kill time, didn't you?!"

As Sora lifted his sleepy head, he noticed around the table *the last three guys*. Nobles in their underpants. Three middle-aged dudes with a little too much fat. Also watching these men as if bearing witness to something very pitiable were several spectators.

—Sora'd been playing half unconsciously and had almost forgotten. But the siblings were in the midst of a game with these three nobles. Poker, *betting everything they had*.

"Seriously, who wants to see a bunch of old guys naked...? Can't we call it a day?"

Indeed, they had just had all their assets cleaned out by Sora and Shiro, these three now-*former nobles*. "All their assets" meant just what it sounded like. Their land, their fortunes, their rights, of course, and even their wives, children, families. All of that had been wrung from the trio in just two hours, and all they had left by now was their underpants.

"H-how—? If we stop now, we won't have anything left!"
"Y-y-you think you can get away with this?"
"If we don't recoup our losses, we won't even have clothes! How dare you?!"
Sora yawned, only half-listening.
"…You're the ones who agreed to play, and you're the ones who laid your families and clothes on the table when we didn't even ask you, right…?
"Plus, if I may—"
As the king continued to upbraid them, the three nobles—no, former nobles—shrunk at Sora's gaze.

"We're *looking the other way* about the three of you cheating together. You should be grateful."
"…Full house… Game over…"
The hand Shiro played with these words meant that the nobles' last resort—their underpants—was forfeit.
—And thusly, the three high-born ringleaders of the movement against agricultural reform were left in their birthday suits, and the demonstrations they'd instigated came to a close.

■■■

The capital, Elkia: Main Street. It was an arterial road that joined the city's north, east, south, west, and the castle. It was Elkia's busiest street, and the one the nobles who had lost even their underpants opposing Sora's agricultural reforms had to take home.
"Th-this is just too much. It's sick…"
Walking the well-traveled road home among carriages and crowds, Steph couldn't hold it in.
"Did you really have to take their families?!"
"What? They just up and bet them. To put their wives and children

on the table, they're the ones who're sick," Sora answered from behind her as he walked with Shiro's hand firmly in his grasp. "But never mind that. This crowd... Sh-Shiro, whatever you do, don't let go, okay?"

"...Y-y-you, too...Brother..."

The two spoke with their heads lowered while flinching at all the eyes around them. For two socially incompetent shut-ins, walking on a big street at noon was nothing but torture.

"Aren't you the one who said you wanted to walk home, Sora?"

"I-I had something to do...b-b-but this is just too many..."

Hardly having left the castle in the months since they'd come to this world, the two jerked sketchily, gripping each other's hands harder as Steph sighed at them.

"So what about all that stuff?"

"S-stuff? Wh-what stuff?"

"All the stuff you took from those three."

"Oh, well, nothing in particular."

Somehow putting his brave face on, Sora answered:

"If you're talking about their families, they can do what they want. If they can forgive those guys for betting them, they'll go back. The other stuff, well, you and the ministers can take care of it."

The purpose of this visit had been to eliminate the nobles in the way of the agricultural reforms. Their being stripped naked was simply a means to strip their authority. Sora thought the state could just deal with the assets now.

"Um, Sora... It is my responsibility for not having been able to head off the protest, and I am sorry for having caused trouble to you two. Still, the way you're doing things leaves a bad taste."

Sora and Shiro may have rebuilt the country with one pillar of wisdom after another from another world. But only having been in this world for a month meant that they were liable to make a massive gaffe or two in an unfamiliar culture. To avoid any slipups from this, they limited themselves to dictating policy while the ministers handled execution. As a bridge, they employed Steph, with her thorough education in the ways of royalty.

—Or that's what they said while dodging all the responsibilities of running a country they found boring. In fact, they had said this a month before—

"We'll set out the policy and direction. You and the ministers can work on the details. If there are any assholes who aren't satisfied with that, bring 'em here. I'll take everything they have and send 'em out naked—that's what I said, right?"

"That's what I'm saying! Your idea to begin with is savagery!"

"Don't worry about it. A *reign of terror* would make things annoying later on, but just one or two things like this is nothing."

Actually, if he kept this up, he'd be just like one of those genocidal reds.

"In fact, it's really impressive to me that this is the first time this has happened in the month since we took the throne."

Big agricultural and industrial reforms always caused disputes over rights. Nobles revolting, guilds conspiring. One always finds lame events such as these in simulation games. He'd tossed all those annoying flags to Steph and the ministers to clear. But he hadn't expected it to take a whole month before they started popping up—

"Well, yes...I'd been controlling them."

"...Controlling them?"

"From the beginning, most of the nobles opposed the agricultural reforms you proposed. Fortunately, the Dola family has some clout with the Oluos and the Bilds, so we were able to get them to help us set the stage."

".........Huh? Oh, okay."

"We used data gained from a large-scale experiment on lands held directly by the crown and sowed the spoils among major nobles who were on our side. Some of the petty lords came looking for a piece of the pie, and we slowly isolated the lords they served... There were some major houses we had no choice but to confront. The three today were at the top of those, so this shouldn't happen again. You should avoid provoking them unnecessarily and proceed—Wait, what?"

Sora interrupted the smooth flow of Steph's narrative by putting his hand to his forehead.

"...I-it doesn't feel like I've got a fever. Why does Steph sound like she's smart?!" said Sora, clearly consternated. "Is there something wrong with me?! S-sorry to make you take us all around, but I've got to see a doctor right—"

"......Um, excuse me, isn't that taking your rudeness a little too far?" Steph's shoulders shook, but Sora only shouted:

"But, I mean—you're Steph, right?!"
"Yes, I am Steph! So?!"

Sora closed his eyes and shook his head.
"Hey, hey, wait, wait...stop, hold up...could it be...?"
Like a physicist who'd just seen a real ghost, his assumptions had been shattered. *It can't be possible*, he thought. He swallowed audibly, looking agonized, before verbalizing a notion he could scarcely comprehend.

"I don't think this is possible...but Steph, could it be...you're—*not* an idiot?!" Sora wailed, hardly able to give credence to the idea.

"U-um... Do you know I graduated at the top of my class from this nation's top academy? What are you on about?!"

"But, I mean—look at yourself!"

—Stephanie Dola. The well-bred young lady, once the granddaughter of the king of Elkia. Now wearing *a collar and the ears and tail of a dog*, the leash around her neck held by Shiro as she walked the downtown thoroughfare.

"What kind of smart person would be in your position?!"
"Aren't *you* the one who put me in this position?!"

* * *

Yes, just this morning after Steph got her ass kicked at blackjack by Sora, she'd been informed randomly, "Okay, now you're a dog for the rest of the day," and forced to comply. Given that she was taking a stroll down Elkia's Main Street in that state, it was no surprise, but everyone turned to stare as if having just seen something bizarre. It must also be mentioned that even at the mansion during the show-down with the nobles, *she had been like that the whole time.*

"C-couldn't you think of something better to demand than that?!"

As Steph shouted, suggesting her anger had returned at this late hour, Sora and Shiro thought:

—*Looks like she's pretty much the same as always.*

"...Steph, shake..."

At Shiro's outstretched hand, Steph draped her front paw—rather, her right hand—over it.

"Ng-ghh... Why must I obey you?!"

"I thought you just explained it a minute ago. Because those are the rules of the world."

—The Sixth of the Ten Covenants: Wagers sworn by the Covenants are absolutely binding.

"...Steph, lie down..."

Flattening her body on the surface of the thoroughfare, Steph cried out.

"Ungghh! I mean, why can't I beat you?!"

At this question, Sora sighed with evident relief.

"Oh, so you couldn't figure it out after all... I'm glad you're the same old Steph."

"It sounds like you're using *Steph* as an insult...is it just me?! Is it just me?!"

But Sora ignored Steph's protestations and took out his phone, oblivious to just how hard Steph was actually working. He took another look at the national data he had graphed from the ministers' reports on an app. It looked like most of his reform proposals were going to go through smoothly. He wasn't entirely satisfied with the area that had been achieved for dairy farming, but if things worked, it should prove sufficient for the population trend. Meanwhile, those employment problems were getting better to some extent— Having confirmed these things, he started his task scheduler. Going through "Reform agriculture," "Reform industry," "Reform finance," etc., he put a check to mark the completion of each.

"…But, still, it is just a stopgap…"

No matter how much the siblings employed their knowledge from another world, fundamentally there weren't enough resources and land. It would take half a year for the agricultural reforms to start bearing fruit. Even if they wanted to overclock the hell out of their tech, they just didn't have enough materials in the country.

"I guess it's true—we have no choice but to 'take back our territory,' right?"

In other words. It was finally time to move to *take back the borders*. But—where could they strike…?

"…"

Shiro seemed to understand Sora's thoughts as he fell silent, falling silent herself to think for a long time. Steph, walking in front of the pair with a collar around her neck, was consequently forced into silence herself.

—But she just couldn't bear the looks directed at her.

"So-Sora. I-I can't stand these stares. Please, at least talk—"

At Steph's remonstration, Sora noticed something odd.

"…Hm? Isn't there something weird about the way people are looking at us?"

"What did you expect when you dressed me up like this?!"

"No, I mean…don't they look kind of *scared*?"

Sora asked having noticed something faintly odd about the glares directed at Steph. Indeed, they weren't the looks of ridicule directed at a buffoon forced to walk in costume— Rather, they seemed to be uneasy glances at *Sora and Shiro*…

"What do you expect when the monarch of Elkia is leading around *someone dressed as a Werebeast*?"

—...*Come again?*

"Wait, what did you say just now?"

"Who'd believe that the monarch of Elkia would make someone—"

"No! That's not my point!"

"Wait, are you saying that wearing dog ears and a tail makes you look like...a *Werebeast*?"

In a flash, Sora played over all the information he had gathered so far in his mind.

—Ixseed Rank Fourteen, Werebeast. A race whose foremost territory was the Eastern Union, the third-largest nation in the world. Little information was available, but they knew they had extremely sharp physical prowess and senses. And that they had something called a *sixth sense*, reputedly capable even of reading minds, and that was about it.

"...Steph, please answer immediately."

"Huh? Wh-what is it?"

"Werebeasts—do they include girls with animal ears and tails like the ones you have on right now?"

"...The reason you limit your argument to *girls* is beyond my understanding, but—"

Of course they do, she thought. Steph blurted—"Female Werebeasts *practically all look like this, you know!*"

...

"...So what you're saying is, the Eastern Union"—with a gulp, Sora asked as if to double check—"is a country where females who look almost exactly like human chicks, except for animal ears and tails and maybe paw pads and whiskers and such—super cute furries— fill out half the population of a veritable Eden that really exists in this world... Is that what you're saying?"

Was she saying that the Eastern Union—was that kind of an Arcadia?

"Hell yeah, this paradise is mine! Let's go conquer the animal girls! Now! Stat!"

* * *

Drawing his phone like a sword, he relaunched his task scheduler and started typing: Conquer animal girl dynasty #yolo.

"Hey—wha-what are you saying! Things aren't even stable yet at home!"

Steph stammered at the "mad king" who'd just suggested picking a fight with the third-largest nation in the world, but Sora would not be dissuaded.

"Ahh, hush! How dare you find fault with this perfect *keikaku* in which my private desires and the national interest are perfectly aligned! What makes you think you can stand in the way of my glory?!"

Looking around as if searching for something, Sora continued:

"Which way to the Eastern Union?! That way?! We'll charge ahead; call a carriage!!"

As Sora ranted, the little sister whose hand he held dropped a single soft word…

"……*Information…*"

"Ung—gh…!"

…and shattered his so-called perfect plan just like that.

—Yes. What they'd just been thinking about. And the reason that, in the month since their coronation when they'd declared war on the whole world, *They still hadn't gone on the offensive to this day.* Having this pointed out silenced the king.

"Hrm, rmghgh… Is there no way to avoid solving this puzzle first…?"

Silence descended as Sora and Shiro shut up once more.

…—. Not that she enjoyed Sora's outbursts, but the silence weighed on Steph in its own way.

"Uh, uhh, Sora, tell me why I lost at blackjack this morning—"

Steph, unable to bear the silence, tried to make conversation.

…No answer. Steph looked back, but…

"……………Huh?"

The leash, which Shiro had held mere moments before, was now dragging along the ground, and the two who were supposed to be there were nowhere to be found.

"—Huh? Hey, are you...leaving me like this?"

Amidst the soft sound of giggles, a gust of cold wind blew through.

■■■

"...De...licious..."

A library on the other side of a labyrinthine alley breaking off from Main Street. Before it stood a café where Sora and Shiro gorged themselves on doughnuts and tea while holding books.

"They're pulling it off despite not having enough ingredients...but it does seem the reserves are in bad shape."

Doughnuts they had bought from one of the stands at the square off Main Street, and black tea from the café. But the stands seemed to have lost their original vitality. One could tell from the vendors' faces that times were tough. It was fair to say that this spoke to the whole of Elkia now. Looking at the data, by the standards of Sora and Shiro's *old world*, it would be about time for riots and pillaging. But what was really odd—

"How about you, Shiro? You find anything?"

"...Hm. Nope...no luck..."

"Surprise, surprise. Jeez, what's up with this country? There's something weird about it."

"—There's, something, weird about—"

"—your *heads*, you knaaaaaaaaaaaaaaaaaaaaaaaaaaaaaaaaaaaaaaaaaaaaaaaaaaaves!"

Concurrent with this cry, her shoulders heaving as she struggled to draw breath, appeared Steph (doggy version).

"Oh, Steph. Where were you? We looked for you."

"'Oh'? What do you mean, 'Oh'?! Did you actually just forget?! Could it be that your reason for dressing me up like a collared dog and abandoning me in the middle of the city was not teasing or harassment, but that you just *forgot*?!"

Screaming with tears in her eyes, Steph prostrated herself at Sora's feet.

"Please! Do this one thing for me...just let me *punch* you!! In heaven's name, I beg!!"

"Uh, well... See, Shiro smelled something good and started drifting away. Obviously, I can't let go of Shiro's hand, and I totally thought she had your leash—and by the time I realized, you weren't there..."

"Steph, forgive. And sit," Shiro commanded, her mouth full of doughnut and her thumb up. Sora continued.

"Yeah, well... Shiro didn't mean anything, either, so forgive her."

"You're making me sit, commanding me to forgive you, and you think that's an apology? It's really just abuse, isn't it?!"

Still in her doggy "sit" position, Steph pointed at Sora and shrieked:

"First, tell me why I lost!! If you don't, there's no way I can accept this!!"

"Hm... So you ask not that we release you, but that we explain?"

—...Huh?

"...Steph...do you...actually like it?"

"O-of—of course not! Do you mock me?!"

But Sora and Shiro would never miss the instant it took her to deny it.

"Craaap, I thought that kind of thing only existed in porn games..."

What should we make of the unjustifiable derision of the one who made her do it in the first place?

Never before had Steph so strongly cursed Lord Tet and his prohibition against violence. The pressure of her stare was so great that Sora had to say something.

"O-okay, okay, I'll tell you... Card counting."

"Card...uh, what?"

"Card counting. To put it simply, you convert the cards into numerical values and count them. For instance, you can make 2 through 6 one, face cards minus-one, and 7 through 9 zero."

"...? What does that tell you?"

Given that Steph still looked a few steps behind, Sora was blunt.

* * *

"It tells you what card will come up next."

"—Pardon?"

While Steph wondered whether this was some kind of magic, Sora continued casually.

"From the cards that have already been played, you can predict the cards that are left in the deck, and then you can *mathematically deduce* the odds for what card will come up next. If you know the next card, you won't lose, right?"

"—I see..."

It seemed the very idea of using *math* for a game was a revelation to Steph. She even forgot that she was stuck "sitting" there as a consequence of her loss to this tactic and simply sat in awe. She took out a memo pad to try to collect what she'd understood so far.

—But pen racing, she suddenly realized.

"Hey—hold on!! Doesn't that mean you were *cheating*?!"

To this complaint, Sora promptly rebutted, his expression serene:

"If you say playing wisely is cheating, then that makes reading your opponent's moves in chess cheating, too, doesn't it?"

"B-but..."

—In Sora's *old world*, card counting was in fact categorized as cheating. But he didn't mention this.

"Cheating is more like *that deliberate shuffle tracking you were doing*."

——What?

"—You—you knew?!"

Sora gave a chuckle and a look that asked *What do you take me for?*

"I've tried it on Shiro many times, though she always catches me. It made it easier to count the cards, too."

Sora, who in his heart had wanted to lose, admitted this with a sigh. Steph, transitioning naturally from "sit" to "lie down," sprawled on the ground.

—Her trick had been caught and, on top of that, used against her. The fact that just pointing out her cheating would have been enough under the Ten Covenants, and yet *she had been defeated by exploiting it,* made Steph weep until the ground on which she still lay was soaked with her tears.

But then a possibility flashed in her mind.
—In that case, what if it *really was a game of pure luck?* Couldn't she win in that case?

"…Heh-heh-heh… Sora! I challenge you once more!"
Steph threw down the gauntlet defiantly, still in the "lie down" position, raising just her face. It was, how to put it—strangely pitiful.
"Steph…after this morning, are you serious? What are you gonna bet?"
It was enough to make Sora reflexively think, *Should I just step down for you?* However…

"The same thing as this morning—that *you get a life!*"
(*Immediately.*) "All right, then."
The nature of her wager vaporized his drop of compassion.
"…Brother, the game…"
"Shiro!! Do you think there's a one-in-a-million chance your brother might lose to Steph?! Hmmm?!"
"…I'll put it…on the one-in-a-billion-trillion…chance."
That was the siblings for you—no, anyone could see it—but they could see through everything.
"…I'll play, too… As Blank…we accept."

—That meant. She wasn't just facing one of them, but the whole and true "greatest gamer among Immanity." But whatever, thought Steph. Skill was irrelevant in a game of pure luck. The odds were always fifty-fifty!
"…Steph, if you lose…you'll obey…one command from me."
Steph must not have seen it. Within the vacant face of one half of the greatest gamer among Immanity. The fire, blazing bright, deep within her eyes.
"Heh-heh, that's quite all right. Now, it's time: the game—!!"

Steph pointed violently to the street corner.

"Whether the next person to come around the corner will be male or female—you must guess!"

After thinking for a moment about the game, Shiro answered:

"…Best…out of…ten. *Aschente.*"

"Perfect! *Aschente!*"

At Steph's enthusiasm, Sora gazed at Steph with hollow eyes and a grand sigh.

"H-how—how, how could it beee?!"

The result……nine versus one. As hardly bears mentioning, Steph lost disgracefully.

"It's—it's impossible! What did you do to score 90 percent in a game of luck?!"

Sora, who in his heart had wanted to lose, explained wearily as if his heart had been torn out.

"—You think people go around that corner for no reason?"

"…Huh?"

"While having tea here, I watched who walked this road and at what intervals. Using the trends I observed, Shiro was able to apply the sex ratio of the population masses in this area by time frame, as well as the employment rates, occupational demographics, etc., to deduce the sex ratio as judged by *the reason they would travel this way.*"

"…V."

—Shiro, having accomplished all this *with just memorized data and mental calculation*, held up two fingers for victory. At that V sign, Steph finally started to sense a certain hostility…but first and foremost—

"A-a-aren't you just like children?!"

Exactly how far did they intend to take a dumb game of guessing the sex of the next person to come around the corner?!

—But when it came to Sora and Shiro, that was a foolish question. The answer: the same distance they took every game—*all the way.*

＊　＊　＊

"...And now..."

The victorious Shiro made her demand, according to the wager.

"All your undies...belong to us..."

"—Hungh?!"

"Wha-what was that?!"

But the wager by the Covenants had already been pronounced.

"Errrk! Wai—p-please, anything but that!"

The Sixth of the Ten Covenants: Wagers sworn by the Covenants (*Aschente*) are *absolutely binding*. The Covenants were absolute—none could defy their power. Though Steph protested as she removed her panties, Shiro exhibited zero engagement and took them unceremoniously. Therewith—the picture of Steph sitting on all fours, face beet red, with no panties was complete. But then the one who panicked most was Sora.

"Hey—my—my sister! Don't you think this is a little over the line?!"

"...I'm...e-leven...just a kid...so, I dunno."

With these words, Shiro placed Steph's panties over her own head. Still expressionless, she placed her index finger on her cheek and tilted her head with a *clunk*.

"Wha—you're going to write this off as *the innocent play of a child*?! Your selective use of that is too glaring to look at!"

Now it was more the young girl with panties on her head who attracted the attention of passersby. Which meant, ultimately, Steph's panties being exposed to the public... *U-unbelievable*. She was one kid you didn't want to mess with—that Shiro! Feeling uneasy about his sister's uncharacteristic lack of mercy, Sora asked:

"H-hey, you're, like, going all out today, huh? Are you in a bad mood for some reason?"

"...Not...in particular?"

But Steph's challenge to Sora itself was at the root of her displeasure. Shiro delivered her response with half-closed eyes and an apparent lack of interest.

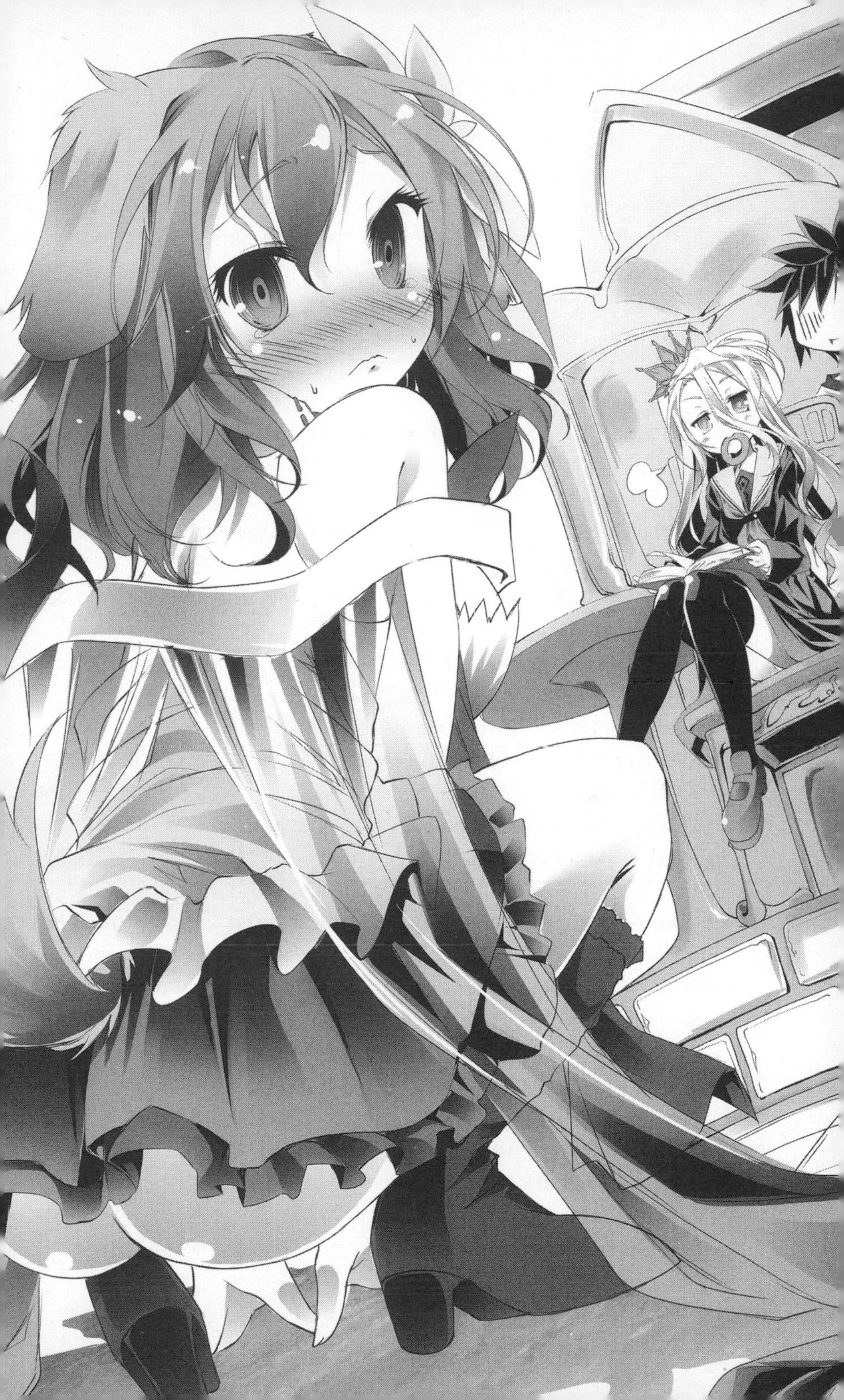

* * *

Steph's counterattack against Sora, who'd commanded her, "Fall in love with me," wasn't "Rescind the command," but "Become a decent person." There were conclusions to be drawn from this.

…You'd think one would be able to figure it out with a little bit of thought.

"…*Hff*…"

It seemed the eleven-year-old girl who moodily returned to her book was the only one who noticed.

—Meanwhile, Steph was dressed up as a dog with her panties pillaged and displayed to the public.

"Heh, heh-heh… I don't care… I gave up on my modesty the day I lost to Sora…"

Father, Mother, Grandfather… Your Stephanie has been sullied. *Heh-heh, huh-huh-huh-huh*, Steph laughed, and Sora winced.

"Uh, you know, Shiro, I really don't feel right about this—I mean, looking at her makes me depressed."

"…It's okay…"

It wasn't clear what was okay, but that was what Shiro declared, panties still on her head.

Suddenly, though, as she lay on the ground wet with her tears, holding her skirt down, another thought occurred to Steph. It was strange—there *had to be such a thing* as a game of pure luck in this world. (That's right. Even just now…they had failed at least once!) In other words—guesses were just guesses. Shiro had specified "Best out of ten" because *they could lose*. Which meant—!

"So-So-Sora! I-I-I have a new game for you!!"

Faltering, apparently unwilling to stand up without panties, Steph sounded desperate.

"S-sure, but…are you really okay?"

Already dehumanized and deprived of underwear, if Steph tried to double down now, wouldn't it totally be R-18—? But Steph pressed her attack forcefully.

"It is no matter!! All temporary setbacks stand insignificant before the cause of revealing your hand!!"

—What was it? Somewhere, there was a hint of why Elkia had been reduced to this state.

"…I-I see. So, same wagers. What's the game?"

"How many seconds will it take till that bird takes flight. Closest guess wins—*best out of one!!*"

In the direction Steph resolutely indicated with her finger:

"Cwoop-*coo*."

A nasty white pigeon sat on a roof. *"Blank can't lose," but in a single round of luck—just you wait!* In all likelihood, *they'd refuse the match.* But even that was enough if she could find a weakness to exploit—! Steph found her expectations betrayed by Sora's casual acceptance.

"Sure thing. I'll let you guess first. *Aschente*—so, how many seconds?"

"Uh, yeah, *aschente*…w-well—*thirty seconds*, I say!"

Though momentarily flummoxed at having been so completely off base, Steph recovered.

—It seemed very unlikely that the pigeon would stay there for more than a minute. This meant that, early or late, the easiest approximation was the value in the middle. Racking her brains, this was the conclusion Steph reached. But as if *he wasn't even listening,* Sora fiddled with a stone in his hand and made his own guess.

"Then I say—*three seconds.*"

He'd hardly finished speaking when he swung his arm over his head and threw.

"—What?!"

The stone, pitched with all Sora's might, zipped right past the pigeon. The bird, startled—flapped away.

"…Done… Brother wins."

At Shiro, panties still on her head, who pronounced the victor without lifting her eyes from her book, Steph raised her voice in furious argument.

"H-h-wait a minute!! How is that not cheating?!"

Of course, Sora was already well prepared for her objection.

"When did we set a rule that *you can't intentionally make the pigeon take off*?"

"Wha—"

"This is what happens when you don't carefully delineate the rules of the game."

S-so childish—just how childish can these two be?! But Sora, reclining again in his chair and returning to his book, advised seriously:

"—There's *no such thing as luck* in this world."

"…Huh?"

—*No such thing*? Steph furrowed her eyebrows at the irreconcilable cognitive dissonance.

"Rules, premises, wagers, psychology, skill levels, timing, conditions… All these 'invisible variables' determine the outcome of the game *before it even begins*. There's no such thing as luck."

—*Luck*. It was just another name for an *unpredictable fate*, dictated by invisible variables.

"For example, let's see…imagine a card facedown."

Without diverting his eyes from the book, Sora continued his lecture adroitly.

"What's the probability that it's the ace of spades?"

"…Uh, there are fifty-two cards in a deck, so one in fifty-two, right?"

"Sure, that's the typical way of looking at it. But what if the card is the one from *the bottom of a new deck of cards*, fresh from the box?"

"…Huh?"

"New decks are pretty much always in the same order. So, if you take out the jokers and then take the deck out and lay it facedown, dealing the card at the bottom of the deck, it's always going to be the ace of spades."

"Uh, b-but…"

That's— Steph tried to argue, but Sora—

"That's right. I never said it was a new deck fresh from the box—i.e., you *didn't know!*"

—went on to explain that that was precisely the point.

"That's the thing. If you know, 1.92 percent becomes 100 percent. So those who don't know bitch that they got *bum luck*, while those who know are *fated* to seize the victory."

Sora concluded:

"You got it? That's the trick to winning at games. The reason you lost to me at blackjack. And, by the way, also *the reason Immanity has been losing hand over fist—*"

And then—with a sour face and a cluck, Sora said:

"—and the reason we're trapped."

……Huh? *Trapped?*

"In the past month, we've gone through every damn book in the country, and I gotta say, you don't know shit about other races—or countries, you could say. We can't find an opening. For God's sake, what is wrong with this country—?"

"Uh, if I may… What do you mean?"

"—What, did you think all we were doing in this month was sitting in our room and playing games?"

"Yes, that is exactly and precisely what I thought," said Steph, loud and clear without a moment's hesitation.

"Well, whatever," Sora mumbled before elaborating:

"Let's say we attack the Furry Kingdom—I mean, the Eastern Union."

His example seemingly designed to make it clear he'd still not given up on this notion, he continued.

"But practically all we know about Werebeast is that the enemy uses a *sixth sense.*"

"Y-yes…they do say they can *read minds…*"

"If they can read minds, bluffs aren't going to work, and there's no way we can play mind games."

Rank Sixteen, Immanity, the lowest-ranking of the Ixseeds, had no special abilities or magic. Thus, if they intended to come out on top in a game with a race that used "supernatural powers"—

"It's not even a game if we don't at least know something about the enemy."

And yet—Immanity hardly had any information to speak of when it came to the other races. Of course, each of the races must have been concealing such data; having it known would put them at a disadvantage. But even so, this was too much. This was what Sora had been complaining about when griping about the books in the library.

They didn't know what kind of games their adversaries played, what kind of abilities they had. But the *other side* knew Immanitites' specs inside and out—which meant "invisible variables" visible right from the start—and that was a whole different story. If the siblings attacked with no advance intelligence, they were doomed to fail. For exactly the same reason that Steph had lost to Sora—they'd be fated to lose.

"That's why we've devoted a whole month but still haven't found an opening."

"B-but…" Steph stuttered as Sora crossly closed his book.

At an apparent condemnation of her grandfather's choice to *attack anyway*, Steph simply had to speak up, arguing feebly:

"E-even so, nothing will happen if we don't do something!"

—Sora delivered his next words completely dispassionately…

"Look…if we make *one wrong move, it's over.*"

…and they echoed with enough weight to flatten Steph to the ground.

"—Our position now is just that bad. Don't forget it."

—For a moment—though really just for a moment—Sora's face displayed a *rage* that made Steph freeze.

* * *

It was easy to forget, since they hardly ever acted like it. But the fate of all three million lives of Immanity rested on the shoulders of these two. Without a doubt, Immanity's greatest gamers, who had even vanquished Elf, albeit indirectly. They said—they were *trapped*. The meaning, the weight of that, finally became clear to Steph, and it bore down on her such that she couldn't stand.

—If they made one wrong move, *millions of lives would end*. Under that kind of pressure—Steph considered it, holding in her breath. Sora stretched languorously, fiddling with his task scheduler. "—We only know one way out, and we don't have the key. Damn, what to do..."

To be capable of such composure... What kind of constitution did he have? Steph felt the hint of a chill—

—...and then. A sudden shadow instantly enveloped their surroundings in darkness.

"...What? Why is it suddenly...night—"

Sora shifted his gaze—and his eyes popped. Even Shiro's usually half-lidded gaze widened as she let the doughnut drop from her mouth. The blue sky that had hung above them just a moment earlier had been erased from their collective vision, now directed to the heavens. As if a piece of the earth's crust had been ripped away—*a huge rock bed now drifted in its place*.

"Wh-what the hell...?!"

—*Amazing! Laputa really does exist!* The line replayed involuntarily in Sora's mind. It did look longer horizontally than in that anime, but however you looked at it, an enormous *island was floating in the sky*.

—Come to think of it. He remembered seeing an island floating in the sky from up there, when he first came to this world.

...Oh, so apparently this was a familiar sight in Disboard. The only ones who were surprised were Sora and Shiro. The other people walking the street didn't even seem interested.

"...This world has so much of everything, it's ridiculous... At this rate, that 'too-soon' thing will..."

As Sora and Shiro gaped upward, marveling, Steph seemed to finally realize.

"—Oh, it's your first time seeing it, Sora?"

And she followed their gazes.

"That's Avant Heim—a Phantasma."

Now that she mentioned it—if you looked closely—the island, which at first glance seemed like just a rock bed, actually had what passed as sad excuses for fins. It looked...like a giant whale—kind of...probably...if you looked at it a certain way. A question popped out of Sora's mouth.

"—Don't you have *rights to light* or *rights of airspace* in this— Wait, 'Phantasma'?"

"Yes. It is a single entity of the race at Ixseed Rank Two."

—*Ixseed.* The "sixteen seeds" of intelligent life to which the Ten Covenants set by the God applied. Still, pointing to the heavens— no, to "Laputa"—Sora howled:

"You're saying that's an *intelligent living being*?! How are we sup- posed to play— I mean, can we even communicate with that thing?! If it weren't 'Laputa exists,' but 'Laputa talks,' even Pa*u would have just looked at the old geezer pityingly!!"

"...I didn't really get that last part, but, yes, it's impossible."

Steph spoke decisively.

"Even the Flügel who *live on top of it* are far beyond Immanity's ability to defeat."

"Flügel—O-ohh, 'Avant Heim'... It was that thing."

Watching Laputa Mark Two—The Phantasma "Avant Heim"— pass by, Sora recalled what had escaped him in his shock: The description he had previously read in a book.

—Ixseed Rank Six: Flügel. The winged vanguard *created by the gods to kill other gods*, in the ancient Great War. A warrior race.

With the establishment of the Ten Covenants, their combat abilities were effectively sealed off. Still, they possessed virtually eternal life spans and high magical aptitude, a literal city of the heavens their sole territory. Thus, they did not participate in "play for dominion," that is, gambling over borders, but as they had a powerful thirst for knowledge, many of their kind engaged in games in order to obtain knowledge from the world's other races. That is, to collect books. For Immanity, which had little to bet, the Flügel were one of the few races the siblings could draw in, with their knowledge of another world. They were the first race that had grabbed Sora's attention after arriving in this world.

—But having said that...

"...I'm sure it would be a great idea to get the Flügel on our side, but *there's no way we can contact them*, is there?"

To get into the empire of the animal ears—ahem. To obtain the information necessary to compete with other countries, in other words— they absolutely needed the knowledge possessed by the Flügel. But in this world, Immanity lacked the technology to fly. They had neither means of reaching Avant Heim nor any method of contacting them. There was also no way they could make their knowledge of another world public in order to fly there. It was too soon to reveal any of that to Elkia. It was Sora and Shiro's sole trump card. While Sora ruminated and muttered, seemingly stymied, Steph offered, "Huh? If you have some business with the Flügel, there's one nearby."

......——.

"What did you say?"

"There's one. She's, uh...kind of sitting..."

No, wait, wait— Sora objected:

"We dug through all the libraries in the castle and the country, and we didn't read anything like that!!"

"You probably didn't. In fact, she's the very one who tore all the most important books from Elkia."

—Sora, assailed by a slight bout of dizziness but supported by his sister (whose eyes were half closed as she likely felt the same), barely managed to stand his ground and urge Steph on. "D-details, give me details."

"Well… Five years ago, a Flügel appeared at the greatest library in the country, the Elkia Grand National Library, and made off with the entire collection…you see?"

—Indeeed! No wooonder Elkia had no data to speak of! ♥

"You n00bs *bet your intel*? Are you even sane?! That's your *only goddamn weapon, you know*!!"

Without intel—i.e., information—they couldn't compete with other countries. To *bet* that, if you put it in terms of combat, was like throwing away both your sword and your shield. Or, to put it in generous terms, fail. Accosted by Sora's invective which made even passersby stop in shock, Steph stammered:

"I-i-it was my grandfather who bet them—h-he must h-have had some deep…"

Heedless, Sora pressed her. "What did he demand in return?!"

"U-uhh, uh, I-I hear he said that if he won the Flügel would have to j-j-join him!"

—Hmm, so he was trying to get someone with knowledge exceeding humanity's on his side. That was, in fact, exactly what Sora was trying to do. It wasn't a bad condition. Not at all. What was bad was—

"And then he lost and let *our* knowledge get taken awaaaay?!"

Scratching at his scalp and tearing at his hair, Sora pointed at Steph and yelled:

"How the hell do you let them make off with everything?! Didn't you make copies?!"

"W-well, it's…a budget problem…"

"Budget?! What's budget got to do—?!"

To the uncomprehending Sora, the panty-hatted Shiro murmured:

"…Brother… Elkia… Book, technology…and lit-eracy…"

"—Oh, huh. I-I see."

As someone who had lived in modern Japan, it was hard to believe. But literacy in fifteenth-century Europe was said to have barely touched 10 percent. They knew from the data that Elkia appeared to be roughly equivalent. Considering that without mass production technology for paper, making copies would, in fact, incur an enormous—

"...Steph, later I'm going to give you a memo translated into Immanity, so get on it as your top priority."

"Uh, yes, sir... What kind of memo?"

"Drawings for 'paper manufacturing' and 'letterpress printing'..."

But this was criticized sulkily by Shiro, eyes half open, panties on her head.

"...Brother... Cheating, again."

"Sorry, Shiro, but this is just *ridiculous.*"

As Sora input a new task on his phone, he let out a looong sigh. All things being equal, then, Steph, with her whole personal library, was in fact quite the well-educated one after all...but. In this world, where games decided everything—

"If you *can't even read and write*, how are you going to game? Are humans even trying?"

"You're the ones who are weird, knowing six or eighteen languages!"

"Don't joke around! If you're gonna play games with other countries, six languages is the *bare minimum!*"

Hff...hff... Having pretty much finished what he wanted to say, Sora moved on.

"—Uh, okay, whatever. Steph..."

"Y-yes?"

"As I understand from the literature, *traditionally, there's only one game that Flügel play*, right?"

Indeed, as far as Flügel was concerned—the game had been leaked. Therefore, Sora asked purely for confirmation, and Steph nodded.

"In that case, the next task has finally been confirmed."

Sliding his finger, he input it into his scheduler.

"It's our time to strike. If we go now, we should be able to get back by nightfall. Steph, get us a carriage."

"Uh...huh?"

With that, Sora double-checked the task he'd input on his phone.

—Get Immanity's knowledge back.

"...Hm, I think this is doable, too; let's add it."

With that, Sora input further.

"Uh, *Get a Flügel*...yeah, like that."

—Though mere moments earlier, Steph had called them invincible. Rank Six—the *race of god slayers*. Sora, having all-too-casually declared that he would "get" one, turned his indifferent back for Steph to watch in a daze, gripped Shiro's hand, and walked on.

⏻ CHAPTER 2
INTERESTING

After about an hour rocking in the carriage, there was the Elkia Grand National Library. It was a bit beyond downtown Elkia, in the suburbs, after they'd passed what appeared to be an educational institution with a dormitory. As Sora got out of the carriage and looked up, just one word escaped his lips.

"...Huge..."

The first thing it recalled was the Library of Congress in Washington, DC. That was the largest library in Sora and Shiro's old world, boasting a collection of a hundred million books, but the outer appearance of this one held its own. It was graceful and glamorous enough to rival the Elkia Royal Castle. It was so wondrous, in fact, that it made one want to reconsider one's evaluation of Immanity in this world a bit. A wondrous library indeed—and yet.

"...You just let this...be taken away..."

"Nm-mghh..."

Such was Shiro's observation as she continued to sport Steph's panties like a hat. The remark prompted Steph—still a dog without her underwear—to wordlessly hang her head in shame.

"A-anyway! I have a question!" said Steph, her tone frazzled. She sounded desperate to stick it to the siblings despite her predicament.

"Yes, Miss Stephanie, what is it?"

"Didn't you just say we shouldn't be fighting some race we hardly know anything about? Is it really okay to take on sixth-ranked monsters like the Flügel without a plan?!"

…Did she suppose that this was a reasonable question? Might as well tell her. She was, after all, merely Steph.

"…It's fine."

"—Huh? Wh-why?"

"Look… Winning at *shiritori* has nothing to do with how much you know."

"Huh?"

"Forget it. Let's just get a move on."

Upon opening the giant door and entering the library, they were met by a space full of shelves, not only on the walls, but even the ceilings, defying gravity. The shelves towered probably tens of meters among countless faint lights floating in the air. It was a fantastic space, building these elements into something like a labyrinth.

"Whoa…sorry, I gotta apologize a bit. Humans in this world do got skills."

"…Yeah…"

Sora was feeling dizzy just imagining the number of books housed here. Even Shiro was moved. It was no mean feat to collect this many books. Even in their *old world*, there could hardly have been a library with a collection this size. But then Steph explained apologetically:

"Uh… I'm sorry to tell you, but these weren't collected by Elkia."

"…Excuse me?"

"They were built up to this level after it was taken, I believe. I mean…when I came here when I was a student, there weren't even a hundredth this many shelves."

"…What a waste to have thought better of you even for a second."

—But, then, when you thought about it, it was obvious. There was no way Immanity could put gravity-defying shelves on ceilings.

"*Phew...* So, where's our blessed angel?"

Walking through the library of neatly lined books, suddenly, there was a shaft of light. All eyes that followed the light to its source—froze.

—It was an *angel*. A girl, with an overwhelming presence one hesitated even to look into directly, a halo curving through a geometric pattern above her head, and faintly glowing wings, too small to hold a person aloft aerodynamically, sprouting from her hips. Her long, flowing hair swayed even indoors without wind, and each moment, the light was reflected from one strand or another as if it were a prism, giving the appearance of a rainbow. When her eyes opened narrowly and made contact with his, Sora was struck for the first time since landing in this world with the feeling of death. Filling her gaze was a *murderous intent* that felt like it had to possess physical weight, which convinced him that this girl, this divine beauty, could end his life with a fleeting touch. It told him that, though he might run, though he might beg for his life, all such things would be meaningless. (This is a Flügel? This is—*Rank Six*?)

A *weapon*, created by the gods to annihilate other gods—to decimate and destroy. As Sora mused that this must be what it felt like to have a machine gun pointed at you, even Shiro, usually lacking in emotion, shrank back and grabbed Sora's arm. Steph, for her part, was sitting on the ground, clacking her teeth, barely holding back from crying.

The awe-inspiring *thing* alit on a bookcase near them, without a sound, without giving even the impression of weight.

"——……"

Heedless of their speechlessness. The angel—the Flügel girl—opened her amber eyes languidly and spoke.

"Pardon? What brings you *personnes* to my *bibliothèque*?"

* * *

—...At that one utterance.

"Zounds... You just ruined it..." the enervated Sora just managed to say, glancing at Steph, unconscious beside them.

■■■

"Um, uhh, why don't we begin with introductions. I'm—" said Sora, pulling himself together and trying to regain his rhythm by taking the initiative.

—But.

"You are Elkia's *nouveaux* king and queen, Sora-*sama* and Shiro-*sama*, *oui*?"

The Flügel girl stole his thunder.

"...Well, then, that speeds things up."

"I like to read Immanity's journal. Congra—I mean, felicitations on your coronation."

"...She corrected herself..."

While Shiro snarked thus (with panties on her head), she still held tight to Sora's arm.

One might remember that in this world, violence was meaningless, but still. The psychology was probably like how, even if you were told it had been drugged to sleep, you still wouldn't want to get close to a tiger. But Sora was seemingly exempt from this phenomenon.

"Hey, actually, there's this celebrity we know who talks just like that, so, if that's not how you normally talk, could you knock it off?"

Sora's remark seemed to be deeply shocking to her. *What*...said the shoulders of the Flügel girl as they fell in disappointment.

"It was my edgy, unique personal language; someone beat me to it..."

But swiftly her expression changed back.

"With that, m'dears, what brings yeh here today?"

"...Uh, that was how you normally talk before that, right? Why are you talking like someone from Kyoto now?"

"I've never heard of *Kyoto*, but thess is the ancient tongue of the former territory of Immanity; tickles it not your fancy?"

"All right, we're never going to get anywhere if we have to keep playing the straight man here."

"Mngh, I hardly ever get any visitors; and I was so excited to have a chance to display my knowledge."

No longer could a trace of the majesty she'd displayed just a moment earlier be found in the Flügel girl, who drooped in dissatisfaction, her eyes tinged with the hint of tears.

"So, uh, anyway, just talk normally. Okay?"

"g07 17, d00d."

"Yeah, we're outta here." As Sora turned away, the Flügel girl grabbed his pants and spoke amidst tears.

"Oh! I'm sorry! I do truly apologize! I rarely get visitors; please don't leave so soon! I'll make tea! I'll bring sweeets!"

■■■

The library was a like a work of art woven of mystic light and bookshelves. In one corner, around a table upon which tea and sweets had indeed been provided. Since Steph still hadn't come to, they'd ended up rolling her on the floor nearby. And, now, with a formal clearing of her throat: *ahem.*

"—Well, then, rulers of Immanity, for what purpose do you seek me, wielder not only of the Flügel tongue, but moreover of every tongue of the Ixseeds, as well as over seven hundred languages including tongues of other worlds and ancient times, to say nothing of the appurtenant background information?"

"…Ah, yeah. Let's see."

Sora decided he might as well give up, and got started.

"I'll get straight to the point. *Give us this library.*"

…

—A moment of silence. At Sora's words, the girl, lifting her teacup.

"Could you mean that *I am being challenged to a game by a mere human?*"

"Yes, exactly."

Her eyes were warm. They truly made one think of a goddess.

"Is that so? I would have you know that this library is filled to the brim with books that I have collected. Considering that to us Flügel who prize knowledge above all else, these books, the repository of my knowledge, and by extension these stacks that hold them can fairly be said to be *equivalent in value to my life itself*—"

—Those eyes slightly narrowed.

"You propose that I *wager my very life*. What do you wager in return?"

With these words, she filled her mouth with tea and regarded Sora keenly with a fleeting swell of *murder in her eyes*. The look brought a thin sound from the thought-to-be-unconscious Steph: *Eep.*

—But, remembering the Ten Covenants, not to mention the conversation they'd just had...Sora seemed already free of concern as he spoke.

"Books from another world——*over forty thousand volumes in total.*"

"Pffffffffffffffffhhhhhhhhhhhhhhhhhhhhhbt?!"

The girl spluttered her tea everywhere, again destroying the gravitas she'd gone so far to build up.

"D-do excuse me...l-letting you see me in such an undignified state."

"...Gross..."

While Shiro protested, covered in tea, Sora still gave a thumbs-up. "No problem. In our line of work, this is a reward," he answered with a wide smile.

"I-I mean, f-forty thousand... You and your jokes, wh-where could you possibly store—"

As the Flügel girl continued to act suspiciously out of character, Sora took out his tablet:

"This contains electronic data—hm, you know what that is? Anyway, forty thousand books from another world."

"—Wha...?"

The girl widened her eyes as if to burn a hole in the tablet Sora had produced.

"I had this to study for quiz games. But it's got encyclopedias, medicine and philosophy, science and math—basically, everything people knew in general in our *old world* is represented here in pretty high proportion."

At Sora's explanation, the girl cast eyes of doubt:

"...Sir, you claim to *hail from another world*?"

"Yeah."

"Certainly, sir—you lie."

"Uh, wha?"

Why? Though Steph had believed them right off the bat—

"It is true that the Elves are skilled in the magic of summoning creatures from other worlds. I myself have some books from other worlds, albeit few. However, when a living thing is summoned from another world, it requires massive power to hold it in this world. For there to be *people from another world*, even with the power of Old Deus, it would be an extreme challenge."

—Having heard this much. Sora, squinting, called Steph, sprawled on the floor.

"...Steph, enough with the unconsciousness act. I've got a question for you."

"Mm-mmghh...y-you knew...?"

"This isn't what you said earlier at all. You said it wasn't that odd for there to be people from another world."

"I-I don't know much about advanced magic... So there aren't normally people from other worlds, then?"

Sora decided that it was about time to stop listening to anything Steph said. He began to think about how he could make the girl believe him.

"—On the other hand, it would explain how Immanity overcame the Elven game..."

Before he was done, the girl gave him an opportunity to prove himself.

"Might you have anything you can offer as proof?"

"Proof... Well, check this out first."

He manipulated the tablet before her and called up the bookshelf app, then opened an e-book.

"I see. This is a language I've never seen… And no fabrication, it appears."

There was your self-professed 700-glot. Apparently she was able to recognize immediately that the characters obeyed clear rules.

"—I have seen something similar… But, a language I don't know, a world I don't know…its encyclopedias…academic literature… its knowledge, a-a-all in this thin box, f-f-forty thousand—eh-heh, eh-heh-hehh!"

"Whoa! Dude, you're drooling! You're drooling!"

The girl stared at the screen with a waterfall of drool dangling from her mouth, and with a gasp she wiped her mouth. "—M-my apologies. How disgraceful of me."

"So, what do you think about those wager conditions?"

The girl mulled it over a little and then spoke.

"—Well, the question is *whether what you say is true*."

"Yeah, sure. I suppose that wasn't enough to prove anything, huh?"

There was still the possibility that this particular book was a fabrication written in an artificial language. The only way to prove that all of the knowledge in this tablet was real—

"Are you two able to prove your status as residents of another world?"

Naturally it would come to that. However.

"Honestly, I don't know. I'm a virgin! My sister's a child, as you can see! We aren't even clear on the individual differences between humans in our *old world*, so how do you expect us to know the differences between us and these guys!"

In a way, it made him look more manly as he laid it all out, loud and clear.

"I think you're the one who would know more, actually. Can't *you* tell me apart from the Immanity of this world?"

Asked this, she observed Shiro and Sora carefully, comparing them with Steph.

"*Hm*—well, King Sora, you do have a somewhat different complexion from that of Elkia's Immanity. On the other hand, Queen Shiro's skin seems even a bit too white... Would it be all right if I touched your body to check a bit?"

"Hmm... It depends on where," said Sora, proceeding with caution.

"Your erogenous area."

"Please go ahead until you're satisfied and continue even after you're satisfied."

Despite Sora's answer, given decisively and without hesitation, Shiro put the brakes on.

"Brother, R-18..."

"Ngh, ghgh... You're right... It was such an attractive proposal, too..."

However, like a doctor examining the body of the patient. The Flügel girl spoke calmly, seemingly free from ulterior motives.

"All living things in this world have some small amount of spirits living within their bodies. Well, to speak plainly, checking nerve-dense areas will allow me to detect whether you have them, so...?

...*Stare.*

...*Stare...*

Steph and Shiro stared at Sora with eyes cold and half-lidded.

"Hngg... Uh—okay, but my underwear has to stay on! And—" Sora presented his conditions for a compromise. "If you're gonna touch me, then I get to touch your erogenous area, too!"

"Why, that's quite satisfactory."

"What, really?!"

———......

Touchie touchie touchie...

"Hey…"

"Yes? Is the feeling of this touch not to your liking?"

"Uh, sure. It feels good, yeah, surprisingly so."

Indeed, he was moved in a way quite different from when he fondled Steph's breasts. So moved was he, in fact, by this mysterious sensation that he wanted it to go on forever. Having said that…

"But, what is it, this feeling of betrayal—I just can't get my head around it…" said Sora as he stroked the Flügel girl's *wing*, while the girl was touching Sora's *nipple*.

"Oh, dear, wasn't this an erogenous zone for you?"

"Let's just say recognizing that as an erogenous zone is threatening to a man's pride. Let me also add that I was, how to put it, you know, hoping you would touch me somewhere else."

Touchie touchie touchie…

"Mm, please don't touch me so precisely. I'll start making strange sounds."

"……Hmm." Sora, in light of her state, glanced at Shiro.

"My sister, I am only touching her wing. Is this not true?"

"…Mm, totally wholesome…"

The siblings' harmony was what was called "breath of *om*." Before Sora had to say anything, Shiro took out her smartphone and aimed her camera.

"Well, I guess now I might as well show my uber skills at touch-based porn games."

Upon his words, Sora slid his fingers, *shk shk shk*, from the base of her wing. In the middle of this trajectory, for an instant, the wing jumped lightly. Sora then focused on this one spot, trying out different levels of pressure, using both hands, at multiple points.

"Yagh! *Uh*—ngh… I a-pologize, but I, uh, can't…con-centrate; please…augh…be gent—!…-ler, if you would…"

"Uh, yeah… Hmm, I guess this isn't bad itself."

"…Brother, angle…close-up…please."

"Oh, understood, Director. Whoop."

"*Ungh—!*"

* * *

"What are these siblings doing to a Flügel...?"

The idea that the two would sexually harass even a *god-slaying weapon* was starting to become something akin to respect in the eyes of Steph as she murmured, appalled. Thus, this process of confirmation continued until the Flügel girl slumped to the ground...

■■■

"Ahem, now, first of all—" Fixing her clothes as she got back in her chair, she recomposed her reddened face. "I do humbly beg your forgiveness for lumping you together with the lowly Immanities, without so much as the courtesy of introducing myself. My name is Jibril. It is my pleasure to make your acquaintance."

"Jibreel," as the Flügel girl called herself, lowered her head deeply.

"...Steph."

"Uh, yes. What is it?"

"...Just how low is Immanity's status in this world?"

"...If we're being generous—rock-bottom, I suppose."

Thereupon, with an excellent smile, the Flügel girl—Jibril added:

"If I may. I understand them best as 'neat monkeys who can talk'!"

Jibril spoke with a perfect smile, devoid of malice.

"Oh, and, for the record, I have no interest in ordinary Immanities. I have already learned all about them and read more than my fill of their literature. Ah...you...your name was *Zepef*, yes?"

"It's *Steph*! Wait, no, it's Stephanie Dola!"

"Well, it doesn't really matter; I'll just call you little Dora."

"What?!"

"Dora, you are of no interest to me, so would you please go find a place to entertain yourself?" Jibril uttered this, too, free from any malice.

"...I can cry now, right?" Steph, forced to dress as a dog (*sans* panties), was on the verge of breaking through the dams on her tear ducts.

"...Well, looking at the current state of Immanity in this world, it's hard to argue, really..."

However, the manner of Jibril's apology caused Sora to express doubt.

"But were you saying that we're *not Immanities*?"

"No, it's... I can't sense any spirits from your bodies at all."

She sparked a small light from her finger to show them a "spirit" or something.

"If you do have spirits, they must not be detectable by any means known to me... In other words, you two do not even fall under the definition of 'living beings' in this world—but, structurally, you clearly seem to be Immanities."

So...what?

"...Then what...?"

To the mumbling Shiro, Jibril flashed her eyes brilliantly and cried:

"You are *the unknown*!!"

"Oh, could there be anything more sublime in this world than the unknown!" Her hands clasped together, she looked to the ceiling as if praying and continued wildly. "The unknown—*that which is not yet known*! It constitutes not existing knowledge, but the raw ore from which knowledge not yet existing in this world is born! I deeply apologize for my impropriety in equating this with mere Immanity!"

—In theory, Sora was human, but it was extremely complicated.

"—Okay, whatever, so we've proved to you we're from another world, right?"

"Oh, yes. With that—you request a game, yes?"

"Yeah."

"Of course, I accept. The wager—" said Jibril, then after a moment of lag: "—Eh? What was it, now?"

"......Weren't you even listening?"

"P-pardon me… It seems the reward was so great that I lost track of everything that came before it—"

To the silently squinting Sora, Jibril spoke in a panic.

"D-do excuse me! For my wager—how is 'all I have'?!"

"What?!" The leap from the mere "Hand over the library" caused Steph to raise her voice.

Sora too couldn't help but think himself, … *What, seriously?* He decided to look on without saying anything, since he apparently stood to gain even more than he expected.

"Y-you might not guess it, but I am in fact among the leaders of Avant Heim. I am the agent plenipotentiary for several dozen Flügel. It does distress me that I cannot wager the entire country, but, well, what do you think?"

…Now this…was unexpected. He'd just demanded she hand over everything in the library. He had also planned *to get Jibril herself*, but—.

"I-is it not enough? Of course, of course it isn't. This is forty thousand otherworldly books we're discussing, after all. Can you wait a bit? I'll go seize control of the Avant Heim government and come back with all of Flügel within my grasp! In the meantime, please don't give—"

"Um, how long is that going to take?"

"W-well you might ask… I-I'll try my best to finish in a hundred years!"

"We're gonna die of old age!"

"Oh… How fleeting is Immanity…"

But this…was even more than he'd thought. —A most welcome miscalculation. I'd better modify my plans…

Sora mumbled to himself, getting those eyes—the eyes he got when he was making some diabolical calculation or another.

"—Nah, you don't have to do that. All I'm asking for is *all of your rights as an individual.*"

"Wha… Y-you'd be satisfied with *something so insignificant as that*?!"

Lighting up her eyes as if flying to him, Jibril.

"Of course, I accept with pleasure! Oh, and may I add an additional request for when I win?"

"Yeah?"

"Can you come for tea even just now and then? I would love to know more about you two. You know—all the way to the nooks and crannies… Geh-heh, eh-heh-heh-heh…"

Jibril's face, at first a fresh smile. Then gradually transforming into that of a dirty old man. It did make Sora think, honestly, that he should have recorded it on his phone. But anyway.

"—You talk as if you've already won."

"Yes, I apologize, but I shall win."

Ah, so she thought she could bet anything because she'd definitely win. Sora responded with a smile.

"Huh. Then we're gonna add a request when we win, all right?"

"Certainly! It's not as if you will, but please request whatever you wish."

—Sooo. Now there was a hole bigger than ever imagined. Yes, quite a big hole—for *taking over the world*. The only one who noticed Sora's thin smirk, still, was Shiro.

■■■

The party made their way to the game venue: the center of the library, walking through the maze of books in the fantastic stacks. On the way, a question popped up, and Sora voiced it.

"Hey, why did you take over this library? It's *just* Immanity's knowledge, right?"

"Oh, yes, well, my home country, Avant Heim, lies on the back of a Phantasma—"

Sora remembering Lapu—no, the city of the heavens that had passed over his head.

"We need no food and live all but eternally, so territory is hardly a concern to us, but then, we have been collecting knowledge for thousands of years, so you see, we do run out of space to store books."

"......Uh-huh."

"And so a draft law called 'Let's Eliminate Book Redundancy' arose in the Council."

—This government Jibril had been mentioning was known, if memory served, as the Council of Eighteen Wings: the central authority of Flügel, composed of eight representatives and one agent plenipotentiary.

"The notion was to share knowledge—and that's all very well. But what it came down to was obliging each Flügel to lend books to each other. *Madness.*"

Clenching a fist and growing passionate, Jibril.

"Of course I opposed it! Four of the legislators including myself violently objected, and yet the Council split four to four, whereupon the Alipotentiary, who holds the right to final decision, allowed this loathsome proposal to pass."

She drooped in dismay, *but then*—continued.

"As I could never accept such a thing, I flew off on my own to establish my own library."

"—And that's why the linchpin of Immanity's knowledge and wisdom was taken..."

At Sora's soft jibe, Jibril raised a fierce cry.

"But my books! It is my passion to keep my books organized and in pristine condition, even going so far as to control the surrounding temperature and humidity, and now I must allow them to be bent, folded, and sullied?! Impossible! Unacceptable!! If it weren't for that little wretch Tet and his prohibition against the use of force, their heads would be fly—Oh, here we are. This is it!"

"Ooh, this girl is scary."

"—Just so you know, Sora..." said Steph to Sora, who had spoken his mind.

"The livelihood of Flügel today rests in collecting knowledge, but in the old days—"

But Jibril cut her off and answered herself. "Yes, before the Ten Covenants, we liked to collect *heads*."

With an innocent smile as if looking back on old, fond memories.

"Ah, how young I was then—sallying forth to decapitate Gigants and Dragonias and such and having great fights about where to hang their heads. Oh, don't worry; there were so many Immanity heads, they were rarity level zero."

Having unconsciously covered his neck, Sora spoke.

"—*Flügel* is a misleading name. You should change it."

It made them sound like angels. This was the work of devils.

In the center of the library was a great circular space encircled by bookshelves. On the round table in the center was inscribed a complex geometrical pattern, and two chairs sat at either side.

"The game, as you may know, is *shiritori*... However—we use these."

Jibril softly extended her hand over the round table. The geometric pattern on the table cast light, and, converging toward the center, countless magic circles floated up, and a crystal was formed, floating in the air in front of each of the two facing chairs.

"...What's this?"

"It's the *game device* for *Materialization Shiritori*."

Please take a seat, she indicated. Sora sat, and Jibril sat across from him.

"Flügel is a war race—ordinary games are not our specialty, nor, if I may add, *of any interest to us*."

"—Despite the Ten Covenants?"

"Yes, you see, playing such petty little games, we cannot help but think, 'Oh, if only we could get this over with by slicing off this vile fellow's head'... These cumbersome rules are all thanks to that devious little brat; someday, I'll fu—Oh, my, I nearly uttered a most vulgar word. Please excuse me!"

""""Ooh, this race is scary!""""

Jibril *tee-hee-hee*-ed cutely as the faces of the three strained.

"That said, there are times when we have disagreements among Flügel. This is the game we use in such situations." Jibril touched the crystal floating in the air. "The rules are simple. We take turns saying words that start with the end of the previous word."

This really was just *shiritori*—but.

"A party loses upon repeating a word that has already been used, failing to answer in thirty seconds, or being unable to continue."

Flashing a smile, Jibril further explained:

"'The more knowledgeable shall win'—this is the solution upon which we who live to collect knowledge have arrived!"

"...Hmm, and are the words allowed to be in *any language*?"

"Yes; however, things that do not exist, are made up, or lack an image are not eligible for realization. In other words, nonsense words and ideas will not be recognized, so please take care."

But, having heard those rules. Sora found something troubling about the loss conditions.

"—What do you mean by 'unable to continue'?"

"Well, this is *Materialization Shiritori*—" said Jibril, with a smirk. "If what you say is present, it will vanish, and, if it is not, it will manifest itself—certainly you can imagine...what such a game of *shiritori* would look like?"

...Ah. So, if you said *gorilla*, a gorilla would appear. While this was what he had been expecting, it did sound like a very entertaining game.

"By the way, what if I said *female*?"

Good question, said Jibril's face as she answered.

"All nonplayer females—such as your sister and little Dora over there—would disappear."

"Are you saying that all the females in the world would disappear?"

"Fret not. This game holds not such an extent of power," Jibril explained with bashful mirth. "We merely move temporarily to a virtual space in which words materialize or dematerialize."

...Merely? It sounded like kind of a big deal. At any rate, Jibril continued. "It is not possible to *act directly* upon the other player to thereby make them unable to continue the game."

"*Upon the other player*, right?"

"Quite right."

"Okay, Shiro. C'mere, c'mere."

Tmp, tmp, pff, Shiro took her place—on Sora's lap.

"We'll *play together, as usual.* In this case, saying *female* will only make Steph disappear, right?"

"Uh."

Steph with a face that looked shocked enough to make a sound effect.

"Also, if you're saying not directly? What about *heart*, or *water*, which makes up most of our bodies, at least."

Jibril smiled faintly in admiration of Sora's care in grasping the finer points of the rules, and answered:

"It would only apply to that which is not presently possessed by the player. So, in the case of *water*, all water *outside the body* would disappear. The same applies to *heart*. As a Flügel, *spirit corridors* are a primary constituent of my being; however, eliminating them would not directly impact my continued existence."

Hmm...well, then.

"Please also note that, when the game ends, everything will be put back the way it was, so feel free to display the full extent of your knowledge."

—Beaming indeed like an angel, Jibril spoke:

"Of course, since you are powerless beings, I would also suggest you enjoy yourself as much as you can *without dying*."

"……Hungh?!"
Steph yelled in consternation, apparently just now getting it.
"Wh-wha? We could die?!"
"The events of the game will not be reflected in real life. After the game concludes, *all* will be put as it was!"
"No, wait, hold on a minute!"
Dying? Uh. Hey.
"When you think about it, I don't really need to be here, do I?! All I'm gonna do is be exposed to—"
However, not seeming to consider Steph consequential, Jibril put her hand to the crystal floating by her.
"Shall we—?"
Imitating her, Sora and Shiro put their hands to the crystal and responded:

"Yes—let the game begin."
"…Bring it on…"
"Will you listen to meeeeeeeeeeeeeeeeeeeee!"
"…Steph, sit…"
By the grace of the Covenants, Steph was brought promptly to sit like a faithful dog.
"Gaaaaah! Now I can't even ruuun! I haaate thiiiiis!"
The magic circles expanded until they enveloped the entire circular space.
At that moment, they were transported from meatspace into an entirely secluded world. Which meant that the game had begun.

■■■

"And now, with that, I yield you the first play. Please select the word of your choice!"

"Hmm. Let's see…then…"
Playing with his phone, Sora put a hand on the crystal and said it.

"Then, to start off… **'H-bomb.'** "

—The moment he spoke, a hunk of iron that really did weigh fully twenty-seven tons materialized above their heads. Having looked up to see it, Jibril (and, of course, Steph) had no way of knowing what it was. Even if they had, they couldn't conceivably have understood the meaning of naming it now. After all, it was what may be fairly termed the greatest and vilest error that humans in Sora and Shiro's world had produced, being, as it clearly was, a *weapon of mass destruction.*

Just as Jibril gaped up at it, already, the high-tech fuse had brought primary ignition by nuclear fission—to detonation. The nuclear heat it generated fused the lithium deuteride it carried, releasing light.
—Jibril did not know what it was. However, the instincts of Flügel, created by the gods to kill gods, told her. "A storm of light is coming that will burn everything to the ground."
"—!"
There were less than a few hundred milliseconds of conflict before the secondary explosion. Jibril put her hand on the crystal and formed words as if screaming.

"—'Bú Li Anses'!"
The end of her cry and the final process of fusion occurred at about the same time.
The light swelled with heat. The "second sun" born in this small room in the library volatilized everything in an instant with its super-ultra-high temperature. With a heat that meant instant death and the following shock wave, it made the building literally "dematerialize"—turning everything in a one-kilometer radius to a plain of ash, in a whirlwind of overwhelming violence.

* * *

...The library was transformed into a mushroom cloud reaching the stratosphere, and in the center of a crater, the legacy of cataclysm—

—stood Jibril, *without a scratch.*

"—Are you satisfied? There *is no way to kill me.*"

In front of Jibril's exhausted eyes stood a grinning Sora, an indifferent Shiro, and a slack-jawed, absent Steph. They, too, were *unharmed.*

"You mean to explode on your first move? If it weren't for my 'good deed,' the game would be over."

—Indeed. The magic that Jibril had summoned was not to protect herself. Bú Li Anses, or "Eternal Fourth Guard"—the highest of all seal spells concocted by Elf. She had materialized and cast it to protect them. While she herself...had *taken the explosion directly* without a scratch.

"Good deed? Hey, hey, knock it off," Sora answered with twisted lips. "You just figured that even if you did get our knowledge—it would be boring as hell for this game *just to end in one move,* and you took a gamble on your *common sense* that told you you couldn't let that happen, right?"

In other words—before a *ball of the unknown* materialized something that astonished herself, either end the game proceeding no farther or continue by shielding them. This conflict Jibril went through in the span of a hundred milliseconds had been seen through, and so she smiled self-effacingly.

"But, yeah, I figured as much, but it doesn't look like we're gonna be able to win on the 'being unable to continue' condition."

On the landscape reduced to scorched earth, Sora sighed at Jibril, who must have been assaulted with the same force.

"I am pleased to see you understand."

"So we're going to go for one of the other victory conditions. There are plenty of ways to win at *shiritori.*"

"...Heh-heh, what a fascinating fellow you are..." As if to commence stage two, Jibril spoke. "Well, then—I earnestly hope that you will maintain my interest!"

—The subtext of her words was evident even to Steph. Even with that level of destructive force, they had failed to render Jibril unable to continue. On the other hand, Jibril could incapacitate *them* anytime she felt like it. Easily. Like glass.

This was the meaning of *difference in rank*. The vast gulf in abilities between races: a wall higher than the heavens. Reminded of this fact, Steph drew in her breath.

—Sora must have been trying to *end it all in one blow*. Using his knowledge of another world, probably the strongest attack he could think of. Prepared to die. Trying to finish it. And now that it hadn't worked—

"Don't worry. I'll keep you entertained—'Spirit Column.'"

Sora, without regard for Steph's concern, casually put his hand on the crystal and spoke. The source of power for all races that could use magic, though undetectable to humans, vanished. Jibril was once more surprised by his play.

"Well, I never—you got right to it."

"Well, I just learned this term, and, plus, I've got no guarantee Flügel can't magically read minds, do I?"

Sora's chattering, grinning face bore none of Steph's fear. It was filled with composure—the calm of one who had simply tried out a tactic he'd never figured would work. And when it didn't, he had simply moved his thinking on to the rest of his master plan.

"Or, what, is it a problem?"

As Sora continued to smack talk, Jibril merely shrugged him off.

"No… All it means is that I'll be unable to replenish my spirits, meaning that certain limits will be placed on my physical abilities and I'll be unable to fly. But such things are unnecessary for a game of *shiritori*, so…no matter, I suppose."

But Jibril, with a hint of fidgety unease, continued.

"If I must, I might describe it as…yes, somewhat discomfiting."

"Ah… Maybe like when you don't have a phone signal."

As if his words popped on a lightbulb, Jibril raised her head.

"What is a 'phone'?! Does it have something to do with that thin box you were holding?! What kind of signal?!"

"Ask me when you win—too close, too close, your face is too close! Do something about that drool, lady!"

"*Hh!* I-I'm so sorry…geh-heh-heh…forty thousand books from another world…eh-hehh…"

Jibril was spacing out with an expression like that of a maiden picturing a delicious cake.

"…Brother, this chick."

"Yeah, I know, it's like she's gone all the way around until I think she's cool again—Hey, Jibril. Hurry it up."

"*Hh!* Th-that's right. Then I'll go with something safe—'nag.' "

The same moment, a horse appeared in the room.

"*Eep?!*"

Prrbbth… Steph stepped back abruptly at the animal's point-blank raspberry. But, without pause, without any hesitation at all…

…Sora said it.

"*Fwip*, 'gash.' "

""—…?""

Jibril and Steph both voiced question marks as if they didn't know what the word meant. But, the next moment, suddenly holding down her clothes for some reason, a beet-red Steph shouted:

"—Wh-wh-wh-what are you trying to do?!"

But Sora grinned.

"What? The whole point of *shiritori* is to say dirty words, right? Relax."

"…Hff." Shiro didn't look particularly concerned.

"Immanity slang… No, even Dora didn't seem to know it, so it must be some secret jargon of a tongue from another world, closely resembling the Immanity tongue, to refer to the vulva—! Oh, I feel my knowledge growing…!" Jibril squealed, for some reason calling to the heavens with apparent rapture.

"…Well, she's weird in her own special way, yeah," said Sora.

He gently put his hand on Shiro's hip.

—*So?* was his meaning, which Shiro accurately grasped. She nodded once—*yes*, it was gone.

—If it didn't directly make them unable to continue, you could act on other players.

"This…offers some *interesting possibilities*."

—Sora secretly laughed to himself, which only Steph saw…

■■■

——……

The game had been going on for about ten minutes. Jibril fired off the latest in the continuing rally of words.

"This dusty lot grows so tiresome—shall we enjoy ourselves a bit: 'beach.'"

Instantly, the landscape changed from the crater ravaged by destruction to someplace like a resort beach, lit brilliantly by the sun. Beautiful white sand and complex crags that put any tourist destination from Sora and Shiro's old world to shame. A sparkling coast with blue that could only be described as lapis lazuli: This must have been the image that *beach* conjured up in Jibril's experience.

—However, Sora covered Shiro as if to shield her from the sun.

"Ngaah! It sure is pretty, but the sun is too much for a shut-in to take! 'Headlights.'"

"There's some shade over there in which you certainly may take shelter, and there you go again with that casual slang… I'm not sure what you're after, but I am excited to see! 'String bikinis.'"

Instantly—her word materialized. To put all the girls in bikinis—.

—Well…technically… But Sora roared:

"Jibril, you don't understand anything! If you're going to put everyone in bikinis, obviously you need to *dematerialize their clothes first!* Don't you know how hard it is at this point to come up with a word that takes off all their clothes except the bikinis?!"

Yes, they were indeed all wearing bikinis.

—*Under their clothes*, that is.

"I-I see… I truly do apologize. I failed to read your intent—!"

"L-look here, you fools! Are you just going to clown around or are you actually going to take this seriously?!"

As Jibril gave her sincerest apologies as if Sora's words were deeply meaningful, Steph snapped. But as if he hadn't even heard her, Sora, with a single irritated tongue-click, continued.

"Oh, well… In that case—'Saddlebags.'"

—Sora chose his mental image carefully before speaking to make sure he wouldn't accidentally erase Steph. At his side, a heavy-looking pack landed with a thud.

"Then…yes, how about 'squall.'"

"Yes, Jibril! That's more like it!"

At the moment Jibril said the word—*Whish*, with the speed of a miracle, the siblings took out their phones and positioned them.

The word materialized into a dust devil—a rising, swirling wind.

…That flipped up Steph's skirt.

"Hey! Wh-what is thiiis!"

—Sora and Shiro started shooting Steph together in high-speed burst mode.

"Jibril, that was perfect! If it weren't for the bikinis, it would've been R-18 because Steph didn't have any panties! But even with a bikini, when you look up the skirt, it's, like, pretty hot somehow!"

"I am most honored."

Ignoring Jibril as she responded with an amused smile and similarly Steph as she struggled desperately to hold her skirt down, Sora spoke.

* * *

"And now—"

Sora grinned.

"With this, it will be complete—'*ladies' clothes—!*'"

Instantly, his word materialized—or more accurately dematerialized what was already present. The result being that all of the girls' *clothes, including their bikinis,* vanished—! Of course that meant Steph's, and Jibril's, and even Shiro's—. After a momentary lag due to failure to process what had transpired, a scream rang out.

"Eep—aaaaaaaaaah!"

Steph, face flushed, trying desperately to cover her body with her hands.

—Does this strike you as R-18? But, actually, *there was no problem at all.* The reason being—!

"Haaaa-ha-ha! What do you think, my sister? We are in the three dimensional world, and still there are *no genitals*! Moreover, their shoes and knee socks, which are not 'ladies' clothes,' still remain—making it *even more awesome than full frontal nudity!*"

Taking his Devil pose, arms spread wide, looking to the sky, Sora declared boldly:

"There can be no doubt that this is appropriate for all ages! Healthy and wholesome! Tastefully erotic! But not obscene! For this is—what I shall henceforth name: the Great Wholesomeness Space!"

"…Brother, omega, props."

Giving each other the thumbs-up, the siblings photographed Steph as she made a scene.

"Wh-what are you even trying to dooo?!"

"I said there were *interesting possibilities*, right? Don't you think this is interesting?"

"That's not how I would describe it at aaaaalll!"

Steph shouted, as if she had been a fool for ever expecting that they actually planned to defeat Jibril. This was just the response expected from her, but then Jibril—

"…P-pardon."

"Huh?"

"Y-you seem to suggest—your world has a rule that the nude body of the opposite sex is 'unhealthy'?"

"Hm, your powers of deduction are remarkable."

"B-but the method of propagation of the race is the same as the races of this world, correct?!"

"…Since you're not specifying 'Immanity,' can we assume Flügel are the same?"

While Sora casually breathed sexual harassment, Jibril spectacularly disregarded it and worked herself up higher.

"B-but that's— To say that the desire to propagate the race is 'unhealthy,' doesn't that contradict the very premise of living things, to procreate? Oh, and 'shamrock.'"

Jibril was naked and her breathing rough as she interrogated them, full of curiosity, nearly forgetting the thirty-second rule before she hastily made her play.

At Jibril's assertion, Sora simply clapped. "Excellent. But if you said that in our old world, you'd just be labeled a pervert."

"The instinct to preserve the species is 'perversion'?!"

Shocked as if by a bolt from the blue, and then with an expression of rapture, Jibril's hands clapped together.

"Oh—how fascinating. I want to see this! I want to visit this unreasonable world!"

"…Hmmm, I can't say that I sympathize." Sora drooped at her response. "Actually, your reaction is kind of boring in a way…"

He had been hoping to twist Jibril's smart face with shame…so to speak—sexiness that is not shameful is scarcely sexiness at all. And then, with Jibril's body, like a work of art, it was like, you know, how you couldn't get off on drawings that were too good—.

"Brother, Steph is more…fun…"

"Yeah. I'll take video. You take pictures."

"…Ro-ger…"

"Hey—what are you taaakiiing?!"

"It's okay. Just remember, there are no *juicy bits*, so it's not embarrassing. But don't forget the shame!"

"What are you talking about?!"

■■■

……——.

And so several hours passed. After that, their playing field had become a space for which there were no words. In a junglelike primeval forest stood moai and a pyramid. In the center, Sora sat, chowing down on curry, naked, but wearing a ten-gallon hat. On his lap, Shiro stuffed mushroom-shaped snacks in her mouth, naked except for cat ears and a scarf. And then there was Jibril, who kept getting stripped of clothes anytime she got something on, still naked. Finally, there was Steph, who—

"Eegya#%$L≠†∂@+§&~#↓Ψ∞Å∫!"

—Chased around by a troupe of freakish pseudo-Cthulhus, she looked just about out of SAN. Filling his mouth with curry, Sora spoke.

"*Mnch, mnch*… Hey, Jibril, don't you ever get hungry? 'Mantle.'"

"Not to worry. Unlike the powerless Immanities, Flügel have no need for food. 'Echo.'"

"Oh, I see… But don't you get sleepy? The sun's about to come up. Don't you want to resign?"

"—Heh-heh… Flügel need no rest, either, so please don't be alarmed—

"I still have an *infinite* supply of words. As I would like to draw out all the knowledge from you I can, I'll welcome your company for any number of days, *months, even!*"

—Jibril delivered these chilling words sweetly, while still making it clear that *she really intended to do just that*. They suggested nothing but hopelessness to Steph—but. As always, Sora answered playfully.

"Ahh, I'd really like to greet the morning in my own room, so I've gotta pass—'Outer core.'"

"Is that so? If you are weary, I won't be offended if you lose intentionally. 'Ergonomic timepiece,'" Jibril murmured, before continuing, "After all, you've already given me a fair bit of amusement *for a frail Immanity*."

Though Jibril said this with a smile, Sora frowned.

"…You keep calling us powerless, frail… It's starting to get to me—'Entities.'"

—With that word, the freakish troupe that had been chasing Steph disappeared.

—*Hff! Hff—hff—!!*… Th-thanks, you saved me…

"Th-they almost killed me," Steph puffed as she slumped to the ground. This scene in the corner of his eye, Sora said:

"Well, yeah, you know, looking down from *Rank Six*? We humans must look *just like ants*, eh? But I can't help feeling you may be underestimating the ants juuust a little bit."

"My apologies that you would consider yourselves—*not* weak, my goodness…'Sandal.'"

Jibril's reaction, as if she were sincerely taken aback, provoked a smile with a twinge of anger from Sora.

"If you think being tough and long-lived is power, you're the one—who's *stupid*."

—The word made Jibril twitch.

"You think I'm—*inferior to Immanities*?"

—What Jibril felt for Sora's party was nothing like respect. It was more like the feeling one has toward an interesting book: in other words, mere *curiosity*. To be told that she was inferior to that *book* was entirely beyond the range of her expectation. Regardless, sneering at Jibril all the while, Sora continued.

"'Weakness' isn't having power or not. It means not being able to do anything—like, for example, some goons I've heard of who *can't do anything but fight when violence has been forbidden*, right?"

"—…It seems you are incognizant of your position." Jibril's eyes as she whispered sparkled with what had greeted the humans on their first meeting—murder.

Yes. Jibril could render Sora inert anytime she felt like it. The fact that she hadn't was purely *play*—nothing more than a silly *whim*. "Aren't you forgetting your place?" her gaze demanded. But still Sora took her head-on as he spoke.

"Okay, I guess it's time I educate you—*on your weakness*. Get ready, you bitch."

And, putting his hand on the crystal, Sora—

"Shiro, you ready?"

"…Mm…"

After addressing the nodding Shiro, Sora spoke to Steph.

"Stephy, have you caught your breath yet?"

"Huh? Uhh… Y-yes, just barely…th-thank you…"

"Yeah, thanks for all you've done. If we hadn't had you to kite all the mobs, we couldn't have *won*."

Jibril furrowed her eyebrows at Sora's casual declaration of victory. While a dazed Steph looked on, Sora said with a great big smile, "—So, Steph!"

"Y-yes?"

"*This is gonna kill a little*—so get ready! *Sit*."

"———Pardon?"

Steph, brought unceremoniously to the ground, had no way of understanding what he meant. Meanwhile, Sora and Shiro—*took a giant leap* and said: "*Lithosphere*."

—Instantly, *the ground disappeared*.

—*Mantle, outer core*. These were terms that Jibril probably wouldn't know had *gutted the planet*. And then the word that signified the entirety of the top layer, *lithosphere*—dematerialized the entire surface of the earth and left them all simultaneously falling toward the core that remained. Nevertheless, Jibril took it in stride.

"...I see. So this is why you said *spirit columns*, the equivalent of spirit corridors—to deprive me of my wings."

—Despite not knowing what the words meant, Jibril recognized Sora's aim—to drop them to the planet's core. She'd never actually seen the core of the planet, but—she took a glance at it.

...Central temperature six thousand degrees...surface temperature three thousand degrees...perhaps. If she made it all the way in, the pressure would probably render her "unable to continue," but before that—Sora and his sister would die. Jibril laughed to herself at how terribly full of holes their plan was. Yes—after all, that was what this meant.

"—You're...still trying to kill me?"

Not hiding her disappointment, Jibril smiled as she tumbled. It was only a matter of time before the heat waves from the planetary core left the two "unable to continue," but—she might as well allow them to make the little time left enjoyable for her, she thought.

"I still won't allow the morning to come—'*Eve.*'"

With this whisper of Jibril's—the sun disappeared. But—as Sora and Shiro fell, *they took a deep breath*, and put a hand to the crystal, saying with a minimum of breath:

"...Eighth element!"

—A fierce headache assaulted them all as they lost the ability to breathe. Of course, this included Jibril...but then—

—*To prevent me from breathing...how meaningless.* Indeed—Jibril was a Flügel. Her home was Avant Heim, at an altitude of over twenty thousand meters. It wasn't as if she didn't need to breathe, but for Jibril, who was composed of spirits, it *wasn't a particularly urgent problem.* However—for the all-too-human Sora and Shiro, it was fatal. They would asphyxiate and promptly become "unable to continue."

"—Surely now you see it is futile. Just entertain me a bit longer—*Tetratonon.*"

Jibril, asserting that it was impossible to kill her through asphyxiation, requesting a certain word, *for both of their sakes.* Sora seemed to grasp her intent.

"...Damn...'natura.'"

Sora, his aim ending in a misfire, reluctantly answered her request. *He's more obedient than I expected; I certainly would like to put ground back underneath us to continue the game, but...* Jibril smiled and settled on her next move.

"Then I say: 'aria.'"

But, at that word, Sora *abandoned his show of reluctance* and twisted his mouth. Jibril was indeed ignorant, as he'd expected, of "aria's" (or air's) *constituent elements.*

—Instantly a *pressure drop* threatening to rob the lot of them of consciousness assaulted the players. Having thought that she was *restoring* the air only to find that she *couldn't breathe,* Jibril spontaneously shrieked—

"—Wha—why—hng?!"

And then came regret. At this moment, her Flügel instincts told Jibril that *she had just inhaled a noxious poison.* The name of the poison, indeed, was the eighth element of the periodic table, or *oxygen.* As his consciousness clouded with the precipitous pressure loss, Sora laughed. Jibril didn't know it, after all—she didn't know atomic theory. She didn't know what oxygen was...which meant...

If she couldn't breathe, she'd naturally assume that the "eighth element" was another name for air, *right?* But what Sora's term had eliminated was only oxygen—not air.

—The rule: *What is present disappears, and what is absent appears.* Then, in an atmosphere from which oxygen had vanished, what would happen when one said *air?*

—The answer was before them. A single element of air, oxygen, remained, *as all other gases vanished.* One consequence of this was the fierce pressure drop, fully 80 percent, enough to rob one of consciousness—and another was a space full of oxygen, which taken in alone was nothing more than a deadly poison that would kill Sora and Shiro instantly if they breathed it in—but then.

—Slowly, Sora kissed Shiro.
"...Mm!"
Circular breathing. To take advantage of the rule that this game *could not invade the players' bodies*, the two could circulate the air that remained in their lungs between them. Though their consciousnesses clouded with the sense that their whole bodies were going to rupture from the sharp pressure drop, still, they could just hold on—for a short time, they could *continue playing* shiritori.

Neither the unfolding events nor Sora's actions made any sense to Jibril. But even so, when all was said and done——it was all still *futile*.
"...You think a 'poison' like this...is capable of stopping me?"
Jibril, sneering at Sora and Shiro, still struggling *vainly*. She thought she had already demonstrated that breathing was not so important to a Flügel. Which meant, then, that *all she had to do was not breathe.*

—It was impossible for them to kill a Flügel to begin with. The game was over. Soon enough, the heat waves of the planet's core would reach Sora and his sister, despite all their useless flailing. *I suppose that is all that can be expected—in the end, they are but Immanity...* Jibril considered Sora with eyes like a child looking at a toy with which she had grown bored. But then—on Sora's face as he glanced back at Jibril...
"—!"
...a smirk rose, as if he were looking down on her.

"Shiro, here we go!!"
"...Mm!!"
This time, they used all their strength—*to expel the remaining air from their lungs.*

—Their next move. Checking that the air, sans the consumed oxygen, had been eliminated from their bodies until there was only a bit of what had been "created" left, to wring out the last of the vapor in their bodies, the two cried:

""—*Atmosphere!*""

With this word, finally, all gases vanished—.

"—?!"

Something popped inside Jibril. The gases she'd stored in her body—the zero-pressure environment created by the loss of the atmosphere wreaked havoc as it pounded her *from inside*, as if to rip her lungs apart. Sora and Shiro had exhaled in order to avoid this... But *even so*, Jibril could not be killed. *More of this folly...* Asphyxiation? Poisoning? Internal rupture from a sudden change in pressure? So what? If they thought that the war race created by the gods to kill gods—that the Flügel—were susceptible to the likes of such nonsense, their foolishness could hardly be overstated. A perfect vacuum—in such an environment, the two Immanities would die first. So overwhelmed that she thought she'd make a wisecrack, Jibril opened her mouth—and froze as she realized:

Sound could not be transmitted.

Sound is composed of waves of vibration transmitted through matter. Now they were in a vacuum—essentially, in space. Without the medium of air, *her words could not be carried to her opponent.* One of the conditions of loss crossed Jibril's mind:

—*You lose if you fail to answer in thirty seconds.*

And...the time a person could survive in a vacuum was—*about thirty seconds. Had they been setting her up for this*?! Jibril was unable to hold back goose bumps. Indeed—if it wasn't possible for them to chase her into being "unable to continue," they could gamble on the survival time of thirty seconds and *finish her with the thirty-second rule—*. At the same time that Jibril reached is conclusion, Sora's face came into view. While clinging to a consciousness that threatened to disappear anytime due to the lack of pressure, hugging his sister with all his might, as if to pressurize her, Sora summoned a labored smile. His face looked as if it read, *"You feel that?"*

—*Now I see: truly this is a most remarkable specimen...* After things had come this far, at last, Jibril reevaluated Sora and Shiro. *Indeed, it is an error to dismiss these as mere Immanities—however.*
—Jibril was unable to use magic. That was because she was a Flügel, her body composed of magical spirits in the first place. And it was also because of the present situation, in which her spirit corridors had been eliminated by the invocation of the term "spirit column," but—. *All the more reason—for me now to answer with the fullness of appreciation and respect.* Breaking down her spirits—she was able *to write a single word in space with light.*

—"Erratic."

See how things really are? Jibril challenged, with the word she'd drawn in space in the language of Immanity. They'd stretched their wills, called on their wisdom, honed their wiles, expended their mortality—and still it was not enough. Immanity could never win against the Flügel. There was no way for humans to reach the heavens—it was an eternal, inviolable rule.

...Faced with this answer, the force draining from his arms like melting snow as he clutched Shiro, Sora felt his consciousness was dimming. But still—despite these desperate circumstances, for some reason, the two grinned slyly, put a hand on the crystal, and withdrew the note they had written ahead of time.

—A note that read: *"Coulomb force."*

* * *

It was—an interval too short to even be called an instant. As they fell through space, the air and the crust and the outer core removed, the space now devoid of a single atom, all that remained beneath their eyes was the planet's iron core. The high-pressure, high-temperature liquid metal sphere, sparkling white, burned Jibril's retinas.

—The planet's core…its *iron-atom* core. When the Coulomb force exceeded the nuclear force it worked against, which pulled atoms together, it was an astronomical phenomenon that normally only occurred at the death of a supermassive celestial object, through gravitational collapse. But now, through the loss of Coulomb force, a little planetary core initiated fusion instantly. The end result had been dubbed in Sora and Shiro's world a gamma-ray burst by photo-disintegration of iron—or.

A multiple-light-year star-system-vaporizing *hypernova*.

The war-race created by the gods to kill other gods were able to withstand a direct hit from a hydrogen bomb—i.e., heat exceeding that of the sun's corona, pressure totaling fifty megatons, *oxygen loss and drastic pressure reduction* due to the vaporization of the air, and the residual toxicity thereover—Rank Six, Flügel. The hopeless difference in abilities, a wall that towered boundlessly above Immanity. But a wall that was *finite*—
—and one which the paltry humans were about to climb over.

In the airless, soundless space, still somehow unmistakably as Sora feebly raised his index finger, Jibril felt that she heard his words.

"You think you can take force on par with the beginning of the universe at *50 billion degrees Celsius*? Let's see, Flügel."

* * *

—Jibril did not know what was happening or what Coulomb force was. But her instincts as a Flügel screamed that something incomparable to the explosion she had weathered at the beginning of their duel was transpiring. Something no concept in her vast stores of knowledge was capable of stopping. *A light that would return heaven and earth to nothingness* would assault her in less than a tenth of a second.

That's—it can't—how can I—? But now at last, Jibril finally understood the strategy behind Sora's and Shiro's actions. Before they eliminated the surface of the earth, they had jumped up slightly... which meant that Jibril *was slightly below them.* Whatever heat might come—it didn't matter. Whether it was a trillionth, a quadrillionth, a quintillionth of a second. *The one who died first would lose*—and then she realized: *So this...was his true intent...in taking my wings.* The first explosion—had been a test of whether he could materialize concepts that were not known to both of them. After that single move, this man had already deduced all of the information he needed. It had been futile to try to kill her with heat, or with pressure, or with poison, *but he had known that from the start.* This series of exchanges was just a diversion. It had been a farce to make it *look* like he was betting it all on thirty seconds. Everything, everything was a trap. As Sora's index finger indicated—the game was already over with the *first move.*

Turning her eyes away from the planetary core, which emitted several times the brilliance of a star and was already impossible to look at directly, a single thought turned in Jibril's heart.

—Otherworlders...no, Immanity—is truly a fearsome race.

In this world where the ranking was absolute—in this world where combat was forbidden and everything was decided by games, to think that Immanity, a whole ten ranks below her, could actually—*kill* her. The laugh that welled up in the back of Jibril's mind transected with King Sora's speech which had been conveyed to her.

"…Born with nothing, and so can become anything, and therefore the strongest race—eh?"

Could it be that their hands could even reach the God…?

At the edge of her vision, having taken the brunt of the whole string of losses due to not being a player, free-falling without consciousness, *Steph caught her attention.*

"—Truly, a fearsome race in many ways."

While she wished in her heart that she could watch them to the end, the blaze of the last moments of the planet roared death as it overtook space, and everything went white for all of them.

■■■

"…You killed me."

"Hey. Welcome back."

"Do you get it?! I'll say it one more time! You killed me!! I did not say '*You almost killed me*'. I said, '*You killed me*'!! I said that three times because it is so important, okay?!"

"But you're alive. You know what they say about fighting games, right? If you survived, who cares where your life bar is?"

"I did not survive! You killed me!!"

Rushing at Sora as if to grab him by the collar, Steph screamed.

"Y-y-you—Not only did you use me as a decoy, but you let me die and didn't even care!!"

"It's not like you really died. Who cares."

"Ah—ah—"

It was all she could take. It was finally time for her to let loose the entire stock of her anger at this man. And she opened her mouth—just as Sora spoke.

"But we would have lost if it weren't for you."

"Uh…"

If she hadn't acted as a decoy for the enemy units that a certain someone had raised, then just as Jibril said, Sora and Shiro would have been easily rendered unable to continue.

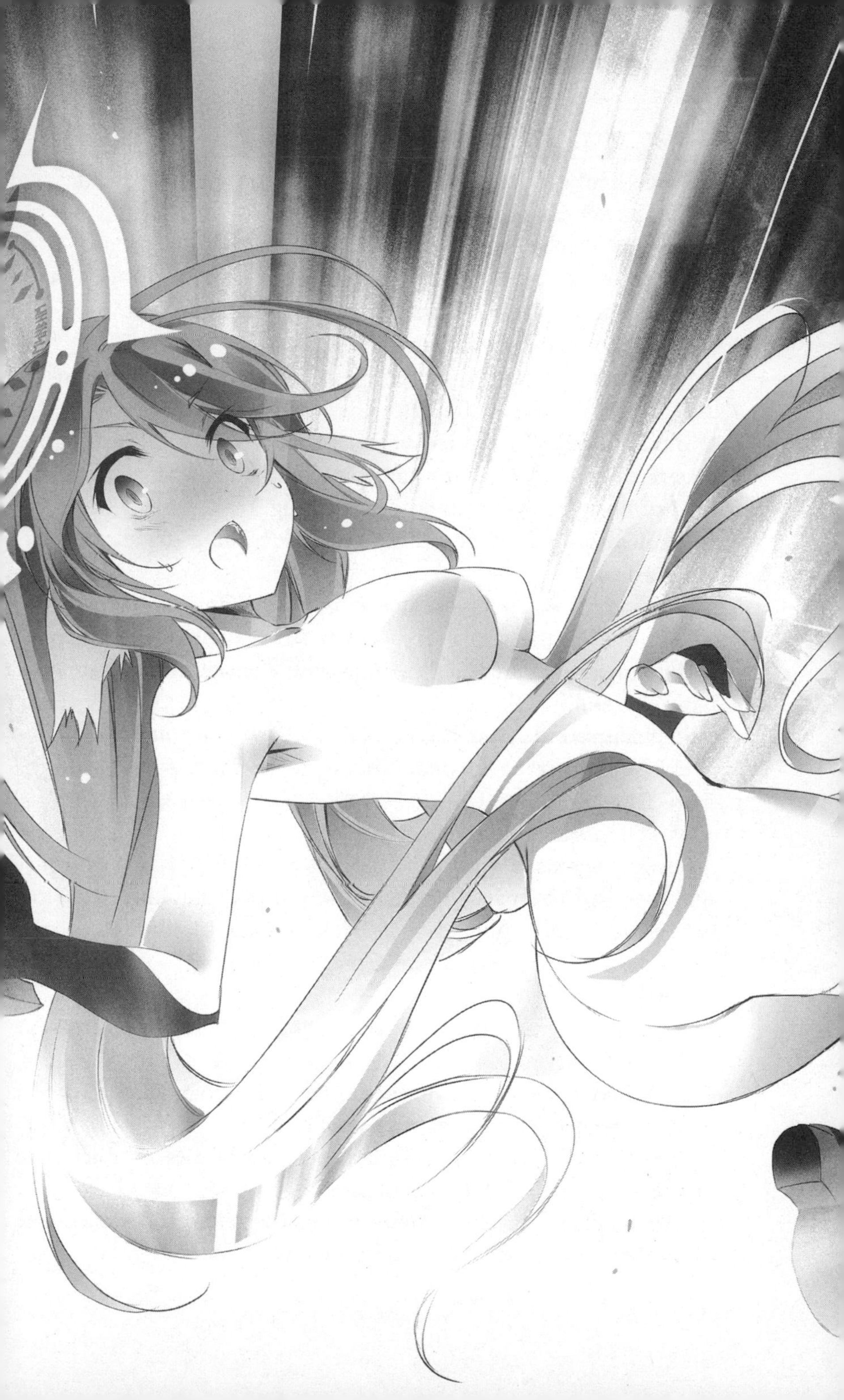

* * *

"And, thanks to you, we got Jibril. You've helped us save Elkia."

"…Uh…um……"

"Thanks, Steph. Sorry to always make you do the hard stuff."

As Sora patted her resoundingly on the head, the rage that a moment ago was like a volcano about to erupt dissipated.

"Uh…um, yeah, uh, uhh… Y-yes…indeed."

Steph, her face reddening for a reason other than anger, looked down, intertwining her fingers.

"Yes…indeed. If it means saving Elkia, for me to go through a little hardship… A-and, anyway, you two…had it hard, too, with all the psychological warfare and…everything. Yeah…"

As Steph mumbled on, filling space, loosening her expression, Shiro asked.

"…Brother…you gonna change jobs…from King…to Playboy?"

"Don't be like that. Not everyone is as easy to manipulate as Steph."

"I can hear youuuuuuuu!!! Aaaaaaaah, I haaate this! I hate hate hate hate you!!"

Steph cursed the God. *O One True God, why did you prohibit violence? Now before me is a man I would give my life to punch.*

"…You have defeated me, utterly."

Bowing her head with a bounce, as if the terror that had just unfolded had never happened. At the center of the library, just as before the game, sipping tea as if to take a break, sat Jibril.

"…May I ask you one question?"

"Yeah?"

"I can see that you led me to answer using the morpheme 'erratic'… but."

Sora's show of anger had been another act, to make her think of a word associated with incompetence. But, still—

"There must have been infinite other possibilities… What were you planning to do if I picked another?"

"We prepared for about *twenty*. But, yeah, if you'd picked one other than those, we would've been pretty screwed."

Though Sora said this with playful cheer, still Jibril knew. This man—in that short amount of time, had read her personality and *narrowed it down* to twenty. But, even so, it was too risky of a gamble. For this game in which he only had Jibril's word that everything would be put back when it was over. This man had even used the time limit of his survival as a *bluff*, and to that, she could only say with the utmost respect:

"You're quite mad, aren't you?"

—Sora took this with a chuckle. At his words—those she'd awaited for the *six thousand-odd years* since her life began, Jibril's eyes widened, and she gasped.

"We're taking on *'God'*—we gotta have mad skills, right?"

It rang in Jibril's ears like gospel and made her heart quiver.

Taking on—God. Aiming their bows—at Tet. Jibril, desperately hoping for the best, but still steeling herself for a denial, had to ask.

"Are you…in earnest?"

Having realized the truth, Sora replied, "Sure we are. I mean, haven't you wondered how we got to this world?" He went on as if revealing a spoiler. "I'll tell you the answer first. The one who summoned us to this world—*is Tet*."

—It robbed Jibril of her ability to speak.

"*We beat him at a game*, so he threw a fit and brought us into this world, telling us to try beating him by the rules here. He's the one who set up this game. We have no choice but to take him down, do we?"

That's all it was. Usurping the One True God was as simple and obvious as that.

"So, Jibril, from today, by the grace of the Covenants, everything you have is mine."

As Sora spoke, Jibril could only gaze at him as if he dazzled her.

"There are many things that need to be done in order to overthrow the God, but there are only so many things that can be done from Immanity's current position. We need to do anything we can to get power, knowledge, and *chips to bet*. Your knowledge and presence will be useful."

—She was like Mary receiving the Word of God.

"Oh, and those books on my tablet? They were just bait. You can look at them all you want. As people from another world, what we need most to *take over the world* is someone with knowledge. If it's gonna help you become even more knowledgeable, we want you to read your fill and make good use of them."

Jibril's eyes were moist, as though she was drunk, but Sora continued.

"Also, you're free to keep using this library to store your books just as you have. However, Immanity needs it, too, so you have to let the academy use it again. You will be responsible for the books. How does that sound?"

At this string of words. Jibril, at last, knelt before Sora. Dropping a single tear, she clasped her hands as if in prayer. No, *actually* in prayer, she bowed her head.

"Oh, my departed Lord. Artosh, thou who granted us life, and now hast none... At last I—we have fulfilled our ardent desire to find a new master worthy of our service, of our submission..."

"Uhh, is that really your reaction...?" Steph, dissatisfied with this turn of events, dropped her shoulders and muttered. "J-just so you know, these siblings are perverts, okay?! They make me dress disgracefully, they make me act like a dog, they're foulmouthed, beastly, twisted, human garbage, okay?!"

"...Steph...beg..."

"S-seee! They even do things like this!!"

But Jibril, already far away, answered vacantly:

"...Do you mean to say this poses a problem?"

"Huh...?"

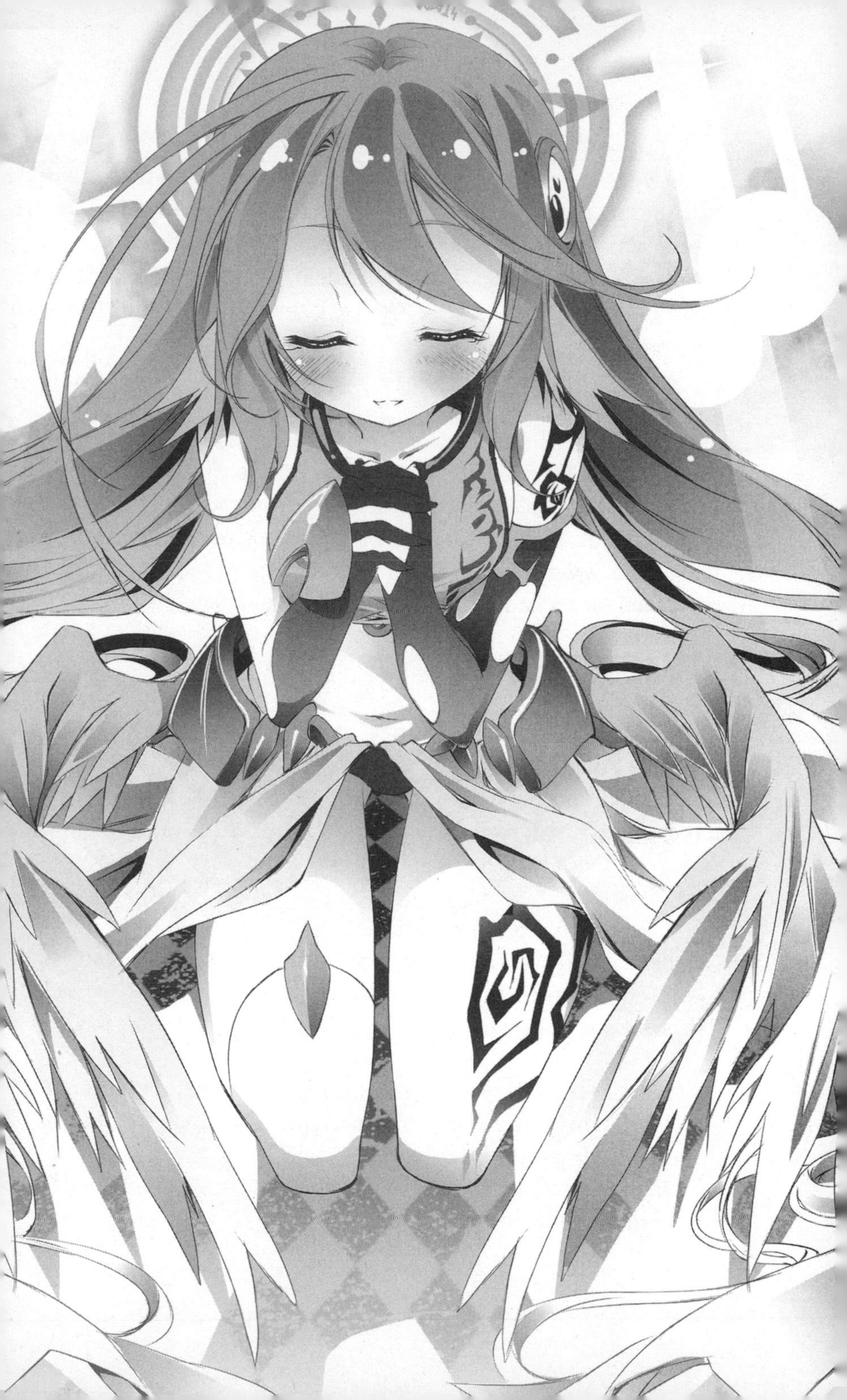

"They will defeat *Tet*, who assumed the throne of the One True God without fighting. They brought vast riches from another world. They, as mere Immanities, defeated an Elf and even myself. They are those who *revolutionize all conventional wisdom.*"

She folded her wings, moved her halo back, and bowed her head. This was a Flügel's single—*gesture of absolute loyalty*, shown only to her *master*.

"Majesty, my master, my lord."

"Yeah, yeah."

"—I am Jibril, one pair of the Council of Eighteen Wings, of Ixseed Rank Six, Flügel." She attended him solemnly, as if making a vow before a god. "All that is mine belongs to you, my lord. Now that my thoughts, my rights, and my body belong totally to you, Lord, it would be my greatest delight if you would use them to their fullest, as a foundation on which to build your grand plan."

"Sure, leave it to us. Right, Shiro?"

"...Mm, we gotcha..."

"This is absurd! Also, just how long do you intend to keep me acting like a dog?!"

Still in the pose of the last command—*beg*. Steph's scream resounded and echoed throughout the library...

■■■

Kappoon... The manga sound effect for bath scenes—yeah, right. Anyway, it was bath time. For today—actually, just for the second time for Shiro since her arrival in this world.

"...So, again, I have to wash her while you stand fully clothed?"

"Don't worry. There are no cameras this time. Anyway, Shiro, get used to taking baths already."

"Makes...my hair all scratchy...I don't like it..." complained Shiro once more, sullenly, with a pout.

*　*　*

"Come on, Shiro. We moved around so much today, you've gotta take a bath."

Shiro had never—indeed, no human had ever—experienced a day as eventful as this one had been.

"In that case," Jibril popped out of nowhere and addressed Sora.

"Whoa! Jibril, where did you come from?"

"I will come from anywhere to be by your side, Master. More to the point: If you have hair concerns, why not try this shampoo?"

She pulled it out.

"Brought to you by Flügel, a shampoo specially formulated with spirit water. Your hair will shine, and you'll have a whole new look, soft and sleek, without doing any damage at all. Quality you can count on."

Sora interrupted the Flügel who was spouting lines straight out of a commercial.

"Wait, before that, let me point out an issue here—why are you naked?!"

"…Mm." Shiro started turning her head at these words.

"Steph, don't let Shiro look this way! It's not appropriate for minors!"

"It's quite all right. I have judged there to be sufficient steam to avoid impinging on these 'moral codes' you spoke of, Master."

"…Hm… Jibril's got skills…"

With Shiro's murmur, Sora inwardly sympathized. But.

"No, I mean, in the first place, why do you need to be naked just to bring shampoo!"

At this question, Jibril kneeled and bowed her head.

"For I, Jibril, am your humble slave, Master. It is the natural duty of a slave to wash her master's back and eh-heh…eh-heh! Eh-heh-hehh…"

"You call yourself a slave when you're making that face?! You *textual deviant!*"

It could be assumed that her intention was to check all the particulars that she had failed to check before the *shiritori* game. But—.

"…Jibril…'Stay'…"

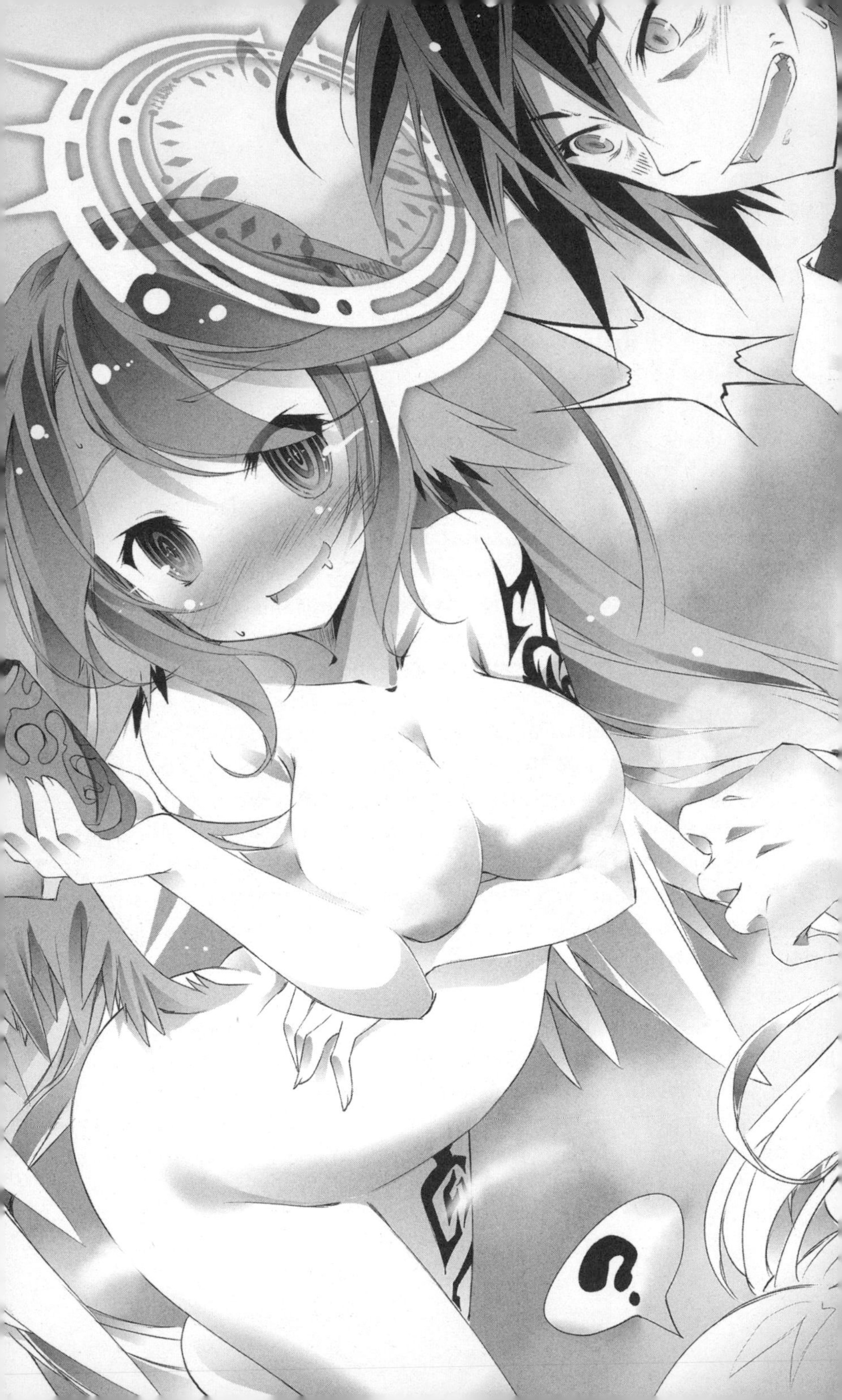
?

* * *

"Eh—?!"

Jibril was forced to sit on the floor on Shiro's command.

"Wh-what? What…is the meaning of this?"

Though she'd become Sora's property and had sworn fealty to Sora and Shiro, wasn't Sora the only one to whom she was bound under the Covenants? But then.

"…Oh, I see. 'Cause Shiro and me share all our stuff…"

If Jibril became Sora's, that meant she automatically became Shiro's. Sora arrived at this conclusion after Shiro.

"…I'll use…your shampoo…but R-18 developments…are off-limits."

"Th-that's my Shiro—your brother admires that coolness you've got. Chills, man…"

While Sora swallowed, Shiro stayed cool.

"…Jibril…you can watch…but stay."

"Whuhhhhh, come ooon! With all this steam, you tantalize meeeee!"

Sora, unable to see Shiro having her head washed by Steph and apparently having learned how to handle Jibril from her, expressed his respect without reserve.

"Oh, Shiro, that's incredible. Your handling of Jibril is really, like, wow… You're my idol."

And so—

"…I can't believe I'm starting to get used to bathing like this. I hate myself…"

Steph felt her humanity degrading little by little as she expressed herself. With a smile, she wept a solitary tear…

⏻ CHAPTER 3
SACRIFICE

A bit beyond downtown Elkia, in the suburbs, was the Elkia Grand National Library. The place had been retaken from Jibril, but remained under her management. In its kitchen, which Jibril had apparently set up herself, was Steph. But her face was one of utter exhaustion, suggesting that she had not slept properly.

"...At this rate, I'd rather they'd just stayed cooped up in their royal bedchamber..."

Sora and Shiro, having taken back Elkia's repository of knowledge, were now no longer cooped up in their royal bedchamber, but instead occupied the library. Steph, busy with the domestic affairs, while also having to come all the way to the library to make reports and even make tea.

"What is it that obliges me to do this... I am no tea lady, after all!"

But, in the back of Steph's mind as she grumbled was recalled that scene after the match with Jibril.

"Thanks, Steph."

—*Ba-bump*, went her heart...

* * *

"It's an implanted emotion! They're just using me for their benefit!!"

As Steph thus screamed and engaged in her new daily routine of digging a hole in the wall with her head, suddenly she was accosted by a voice.

"Oh, if it isn't little Dora. I see you're as industrious as ever."

"Can you not call me 'little Dora'?! Wait, when did you even get there?!"

Though there'd been no sound of a door, Jibril was standing there as if she'd always been there.

"I have a message from my master."

"Oh? Um, can you answer my..."

"Let's see... 'Jibril says there's all kinds of stuff in the kitchen, like sugar and butter and shit. Apparently it's all ours now, so I guess you can use it; knock yourself out'—those were his words."

"...Huh?"

—She could use sugar and butter? Th-that would dramatically expand the scope of sweets she could—

"Hey, they're just indirectly telling me to make delicious sweets for them, aren't they! Just how far are they planning to walk over me?! I'd rather they tell me I could take a break!!"

Bam, bam, bam.

"I'm sorry to bother you in the midst of your head training..." said Jibril, extracting a note. "However, my master has made a note regarding a type of sweet that interests him based on a cookbook he found in my collection—"

"Why, thank you! ♥ I will certainly—*ah!*" Jibril's eyes looked distinctly amused, and Steph flailed her arms with a blush. "No—this is..."

"I have heard the story. It seems that my master ordered you to fall in love with him."

"E-exactly! And by some kind of swindle tantamount to fraud, you know! Can you believe it?!"

Steph, seizing on excuses to justify her actions, raised a smoke screen. Meanwhile, Jibril seemed all the more curious.

"Well, I don't know. I have little understanding of the ways of Immanity love. Please forgive me."

"Oh—i-is that so?"

"Indeed. For ours is a race that only reproduces when necessary. All I need is love for my master. My grasp of the subtleties of the heart to which Immanity refers as 'romance' is limited to what I have heard."

Jibril so casually mentioned her master—that is, Sora—in the same decisive sentence as "love."

"Uh, well…um, by 'love,' you mean…the, master-disciple kind, right?"

"I am little capable of making such distinctions. What do you mean by *normal love*?"

"Uh, yes… It's as if, when you see them close to another your heart constricts; when they're away you become uneasy; that kind of…—Huh?"

Steph realized that her first love was Sora, with whom she'd been forced to fall in love against her will.

She realized, in other words, that everything she just said was about Sora. She realized that Jibril, watching sunnily, *could see it all.* Blushing redder than a tomato and panicking, she said:

"I-I-I-I-I'm only talking in general, you know, in general! I-I don't have any personal—"

Jibril only smiled at her utterly unconvincing defense.

"I see. With that, as I have delivered my message, I will take my leave."

"Uh, all right… Thanks for—huh?"

She was gone. In the second she'd averted her eyes…where had she gone?

"……—(*Peek!*)"

Steph glanced at the recipe on the table for the sweets in which Sora had taken an interest.

"W-well… If we have butter, there are certain sweets I would like to try myself, after all. And, if I'm going to make them for one, it's not much more work to make them for everyone. Yes, yes, that's it. It's in passing, only in passing."

Steph started to rummage through Jibril's kitchen.

"Hmm… The first thing is to figure out where everything is, I suppose…"

"Let me explain."

"Eegh?!"

Jibril popped up once more soundlessly from behind.

"The preparation equipment you will need is in this cupboard. The dishes are over there. The ingredients and spices are on the shelf above. The tea set is here. The oven was made in Avant Heim, but I have summarized the directions for you in Immanity here. With that, I leave you to your devices."

"Uh, um, okay… Thank you for everything," said Steph while shrinking a bit.

"No, it is all in the service of *my master*. Farewell."

Once more, she vanished. Of *her master*… Steph felt a certain edge in these words. It sounded vaguely like some sort of threat, but was she just imagining it? But Steph just shook her head.

"These are…for me!! Yes, now, it's time I prepare sweets so delicious I shall surprise myself!!"

Her mind was crossed again by the sight after the match with Jibril. Her head being stroked—with only the words modified.

—You're so good, Steph. Thanks.

"Like. I. Said—!"

Smashing her hands down onto the table.

"It's not like thaaat!"

As Steph bashed her head against the table. Outside the door, Jibril.

"'Fall in love with me'… Such a fascinating request is truly the work of my master."

Yet she spoke as if she saw something even more fascinating.

Though Jibril did not well understand the feelings of Immanity, she did at least know something about the theory of romantic affection.

"...Love burns in a flash and cools just as fast—why is it that Dora, who has not been ordered 'Stay in love,' should be *affected long-term*? Hee-hee, how endlessly intriguing."
Thus giggling quietly, she faded back into the void.

"Uh—red... Eeyaughh, it's blooood?! Eungh..."
With Steph passing out at her own blood, it looked like the sweets would take a while longer.

■■■

Having rubbed ointment on her forehead and dressed it, Steph carried with effort the four servings of teacakes she'd completed after recovering from unconsciousness.
"Hee-hee-hee, now these are perfect!"
Steph congratulated herself on being flawless now that she had sugar and butter again, then headed for the room at the back of the library so as not to let it be thought she'd come just to hear Sora's praise.
—And found that, with her hands full, she couldn't open the door.
"This situation gives me an odd sense of déjà vu."
Were the déjà vu to continue, her opening the door would be punctuated by finding no one there...she thought. In the end, fortunately, the déjà vu did not continue. Rather—

"So—Jibril."
A man was interrogating Jibril with the most serious face imaginable.
"Will you tell me about the country of animal-eared girls I'm about to conquer—about this *Eastern Union*?"
...A man one didn't want to believe could be entrusted with the fate of Immanity was there.

* * *

"Yes, Lord, the Eastern Union is a country with a complicated background."

The Eastern Union—the country of Rank Fourteen, Werebeast. Though the Werebeasts were considered a single race, it included countless tribes based on differences in physical characteristics. As a result, for many years, they cycled through civil war and truce among a number of small, disparate islands. Then suddenly a figure known as the Shrine Maiden subjugated and unified them over a period of only half a century. Now it was an enormous maritime empire, the third-largest nation in the world.

"Differences in physical characteristics...like, some have cat ears and some have fox ears?"

Sora responded to this part deadpan, to which Jibril answered:

"Yes. But perhaps even more critical than differences in appearance is differences in function. Though they are called Werebeasts, please do not think that their physical abilities are merely beastlike. For some tribes and individuals possess abilities *approaching physical limits*, and such unthinkable abilities allow them to *even read minds*. In addition, some individuals called .*bloodbreaks* even go beyond—"

"Hm, sure, I get the picture—so.

"The animal-eared girls are mine; now, how are we going to smash this Eastern Union!"

—This king was hopeless.

"I'm sorry to say, Master, that it is most likely *impossible*."

The one who dumped the cold water on him turned out to be none other than she who called him Master and claimed obedience: Jibril.

"Wha—Jibril, for what did I invite you into my party—as a sage?! How could you say such a thing about my godly scheme that fulfills both my private desires and the national interest—to pet animal-eared girls!"

Despite how fearlessly he displayed the extent to which his self-interest overrode important national concerns, Jibril remained unmoved.

"Master, I am most humbled. However—I do feel that even the two of you may be *unable to defeat the Eastern Union.*"

At these words, Sora, and even Shiro, who'd been reading a book at his side, squinted and glared at Jibril.

"Mmm? Are you trying to say that Blank will lose?"

"No, I worded that poorly. I simply meant that things may not proceed as planned."

The reason being—.

"I myself have once challenged the Eastern Union—*and lost.*"

...What...?

"...Seriously? Wha, at *shiritori?*"

"No, as it was I who initiated the challenge."

...How many games could beat a freak multipurpose humanoid decisive weapon like her...?

"It was most likely the other party who selected the game."

—*Most likely?*

"If I may add, the Elves—Elven Gard has challenged the Eastern Union to a formal battle of nations four times in the last fifty years, and each of those times—*they were defeated,*" said Jibril, as if stating an unwelcome but inescapable fact.

But more importantly—Sora had to understand what her words meant, and why Jibril had gone so far as to state that it was *impossible.*

"...Could it be..."

But if it were the truth—it would mean, after all...

"...the Eastern Union...demands as a wager that you lose your memory of the game?"

...that, at present, it was impossible to win.

Bowing her head in reverence, Jibril spoke.

"My master indeed is wise. For this reason, *not a single detail of their game or games is known.*"

...Well, then. The race known for superior senses and some kind of sixth sense that let them read minds had gone so far as to erase memories to conceal their games. There was no place to dig; there was no way to learn from loss. Indeed, to challenge them under these conditions, with no prior information, would be suicide.

—But that left several unanswered questions.

"Elven Gard lost...*four times?*"

Elven Gard. The thing was, he knew from their experience in the tournament to become monarch of Elkia what a pain those Elves could be. Even against Chlammy, who had merely called on their power indirectly, he was sure to have lost if he had had no prior information. Even attacking with two or three lines of defense prepared, she had forced them to struggle. And they were the largest country in the world. To be able to hold one's own against that—

"Yes, and, as a consequence—I suspected *the involvement of a higher race.*"

Yes, just as Elven Gard had tried to do to Elkia. Someone else, who could even have pushed aside the Elves, might have turned the Eastern Union into a puppet state.

"And I was so curious about who could be behind it, were that the case—"

"You challenged them and got your ass handed to you."

"...I can say nothing in my defense."

Well, then. That explained why Jibril stated it was impossible. If they didn't know anything about the game and had no way to bluff, there was no room for strategy. And, in this case, Sora's crew, who had no weapons but wit and wiles, was all but doomed to be prey.

—But even so, there was a doubt that couldn't be wiped away.

"...Isn't the one who's challenged at an overwhelming advantage in this world?"

The Fifth of the Ten Covenants: The party challenged shall have the right to determine the game. Obviously, someone who could select the game that suited them was in a superior position.

"But then if they erase all the memories—*after a while, no one would try, right?*"

—Yes. It was like nuclear deterrence in Sora's world. No one would pick a fight once they knew there was no way to win against the opponent.

"...Defensive, defense...?"

Shiro speculated on the implications for the stance of the Eastern Union. But Sora pointed something out.

"Shiro, you may be smarter than your brother, but this is why you lose to him in strategy games. *There's no fun in that, right?*"

If they had an unbeatable move that even beat Elf and Flügel, why would they stop at defensive defense? The real fun was making it look like there was an opening, *getting others to attack, and then kicking their asses.*

"...Brother, your...play style...is lame."

"Are you saying the strategy I spent all my brains concocting is lame? That makes your brother really sad, you know?!"

But yeah. Shiro recognized she'd gone in the wrong direction.

"...For a country...that's surged in the last half century...to adopt defensive defense...is weird."

"I-isn't it?"

Sora, grabbing on to Shiro with tears in his eyes. Jibril spoke to the siblings who looked quizzical at the unresolvable contradiction.

"But in fact, in the last ten years, no country has challenged the Eastern Union to a battle of nations—"

...Jibril smiled.

"—oh, yes...except one."

"...Mm..."

"Huh, what, which?"

Only Jibril and Shiro reacted. Shiro must have read about it already in Jibril's books, but it was news to Sora.

—Oh, this is not a welcome development.

Steph detected an imminent disaster and tried to quietly leave the room.

"I believe it may be easiest to see for yourself. Dora should come along, of course."

"Hngmh?!"

Not knowing when she had been approached, Steph raised her voice at the hand on her shoulder.

"Please hold on to me, everyone."

"Hold on?"

Sora and Shiro obediently grabbed Jibril's clothes.

"And please do not let go—for now we begin."

And, the instant Jibril spoke, a sound at Sora's ears like glass breaking made him close his eyes for a moment—and, just then. As he opened his eyes again, what he beheld…hmm, could it be a trick of the imagination?

—It appeared that he was floating a few thousand meters above the ground; quite a nice view, yes?

"What splendid weather we have today; visibility should be—"

"Wait, Jibril, hold on; first of all—*what did you just do*?!"

Sora interrupted Jibril, who went on as if nothing had happened. While Sora demanded an explanation of this situation in which they'd been launched into the air at very high altitude in zero frames, Jibril answered nonchalantly that she'd just accomplished teleportation. "Whatever do you mean…? I merely shifted."

…So that was why it seemed she could pop up anywhere, Sora realized. She actually was a teleporter. It was hard to wrap one's head around, but it made sense.

"…Just how far can you shift?"

"Anywhere I can see. Or, otherwise, *anywhere I have once visited.*"

—Sora and Shiro had just run upon the greatest mystery of this world.

"—Hey, Shiro, how is it that Immanity survived the old war?"

"......Dunno...?"

If they had a "war" against the Werebeasts, with physical prowess said to *approach physical limits*, Elves, with their disregard for freaking common sense, and insane life-forms like Jibril, did that mean Immanity was actually able to put up a fight against this shit? But each of the *residents of this world* would answer that question thus:

"That is considered the greatest mystery in the history of the human race..." said Steph, with a sigh.

"Perhaps it was simply that no one took notice of Immanity?" answered Jibril with an excellent smile.

"We were mainly engaged with the Dragonia, the Gigant, and the Old Deus. Oh, to think back on those days of just barely bringing down a dragon with fifty Flügel, or when we took on a god with a force of two hundred and yet were routed."

...She was saying that a race that took a hypernova to kill, that could teleport freely, and could fly, had failed to bring down one of these things when they went in a gang of two hundred, *and this was what everyone was waging war against.*

"That raises another question:

"—How is it that this planet even retained its shape?"

But Jibril answered Sora's question with a bashful smile.

"That is exactly *the reason the One True God was decided by default.*"

............................It hadn't...retained its shape after all.

"But never mind that. Look over there."

As Jibril smiled as if to sweep away bad memories, she pointed to a place near the Elkia border, clearly visible from the air. On the inside of the national border, that is, inside Elkia's territory, in the distance loomed an imposing tower. Yes, a tower, imposing.

—A structure that clearly was impossible for Immanity to have built—or, to get to the point...

"...Uhh, what, is that...a *skyscraper*?"

Indeed, it was a building more or less like America's Empire State Building.

"...So huge."

Even Shiro's eyes widened. Their sense of perspective was almost lost, except for the contrast with the buildings lined up below, which looked like an Immanity neighborhood.

"Little Dora, could you please explain?"

Slumping—*I knew this would happen*—Steph spoke.

"...It's the Eastern Union's—embassy in Elkia."

"......Hmmm, embassy?"

Swishing her head away from Sora's squint, Steph continued. "Th-the truth is—it's where our country's royal palace *used* to be."

"............Hey."

As Sora squinted further into Steph's face, Steph turned her neck further back in an attempt to escape his gaze.

"G-Grandfather h-had lost and lost and, uh, f-finally bet the palace."

"...And, lost..." said the sister, softly, mercilessly.

"......"

Sora and Shiro had no more words, while Jibril beamed as if watching a puppy.

"Wh-what are you looking at me like that for!"

"If your *capital* has an embassy bigger than the Royal Castle, that is pretty pathetic..."

"Unghh..."

Hmm... Sora started thinking.

"So how did this Royal Castle get taken by the Eastern Union?"

"More to the point—*everything on that side* was taken by the Eastern Union."

"—Huh?"

Jibril spoke sunnily, while Sora gaped incredulously. His sister explained with information she'd memorized.

"...In, the last ten years...the former king...lost to the Eastern Union...*eight times.*"

"Eight... Uh, well, I can see the Eastern Union's motivation. A maritime nation with that kind of technology—"

The difficulty for a maritime nation was the lack of iron and stone, i.e., resources other than maritime resources. Judging from the style of that building, it appeared they had quite an advanced civilization. There were many resources they'd need, such as rare metals, that couldn't be obtained in an archipelago. So it was only natural that they'd try to get them from the continent—but.

"But it was the Eastern Union who wanted the match, right? Why did he accept?"

However, Shiro shook her head. And then Jibril answered.

"Master, have you forgotten? The *only nation that has challenged the Eastern Union in these last ten years...*"

"...The initiator was...*Elkia...*"

...What...?

"First that mountain. Then that plain, and then...in the end, he bet the Royal Castle that had stood at the center of the nation—and here we are now."

Jibril explained that she had flown them up in order to show them this.

"Hey, hey, wait a second, it *had stood at the center of the nation?*"

Sora said, pointing at the "Empire State Building."

"So what are you saying? That we bet half our territory challenging an opponent against whom even Elven Gard had lost after challenging them four times, and we challenged them eight times? Immanity? Hey, hey, come on. Cut the—"

But, to Shiro, responding with a sigh, Sora still shook his head.

"H-hey, wait, so what are you saying? That Elkia before that—*had twice as much land as it does now?*"

At Shiro, nodding decisively, and Jibril, Sora put his fingers to his eyebrow. Steph had no more words.

"…Jibril, I want to go back to the library."

"Oh, dear, are you afraid of heights?"

"No, I just can't clutch my head here, so I want a floor."

■■■

Back in the library. Sora sat cross-legged on a table, clutching his head. All that had come from his mouth for some time now had been sighs, one after the other. In her usual spot on his lap, Shiro peered at him with concern.

"…Brother…are you o…kay…?"

"…Yeah, sorry, Shiro, I'm just kind of in despair."

It pained him to cause his sister concern, but, even so, it had to be said.

"I thought the old king was a moron, but, God, he had to be an alcoholic or something…"

Sigh……

Steph, who'd been listening, heard this long sigh and snapped.

"Y-you've been rather rude, you know!!" She hit the table on which Sora sat with a bang. "I thought you said before that my grandfather was right!!"

But Sora, with a great sigh, replied.

"—Just how do you defend someone who threw away half of the national territory on some crazy charge?" he said, predictably pointing in the direction of the lost land that they'd seen just recently.

"How much dairy farming and industry could you fit on that land area? If your gramps hadn't gambled until he was in his shorts like those dumbass nobles, we would have had *twice* the amount of land we do, you know!"

"W-well, it's—!"

As if he couldn't stop his mouth once it had started, Sora grumbled: "Yeah, he sure was *your grandfather*… Maybe he believed in that 'luck' shit, that if he kept playing the game eventually he'd win… We're talking about competition between *nations*… Didn't he understand what that meant?"

—Yes, a personal game and a *battle of nations* were two entirely different stories. A game that the agent plenipotentiary, a party responsible for other people's lives, played with their lives as collateral. That was a battle of nations—a *play for dominion*. It was a game in which each race, each nation, would mobilize all the knowledge and strategy they had at their disposal. To challenge a nation that was *ready for this* no less than eight times—.

"I mean, is there a more positive interpretation than 'He was drunk'…?"

But, shaking her shoulders, looking down, and squeezing out her words, Steph spoke.

"Grandfather—it is true…had not much of a head, for games…"

But—she lifted her head and shrieked:

"He was not the sort of madman who would assume the burden of the lives of millions of Immanities without care! Unlike you two, he was a model of common decency!"

But, given the actual situation resulting from this model…

"If throwing away half the territory is 'a model of common decency,' I'm happy to be an uncommon deviant."

"~~! I've had enough of this!!"

Shaking her shoulders yet unable to argue, Steph ran away with tears in her eyes. Watching her recede, Shiro muttered:

"…Brother…that's harsh…"

"…What do you want me to say after seeing that…?"

Sora spoke as if he had many things to think about, his melancholy switch all the way on and the excitement of a moment ago now lost.

—Then. He noticed the tea and cakes Steph had brought and left on the table. Faster than Sora, Shiro took some and stuffed them in her mouth.

"...Mm, good...!"

Hearing Shiro's usually monotonous voice take a leap, Sora picked at the food reluctantly.

"......Damn it, it really is good..."

Sweet, but not cloying, and so fluffy. Though they had eaten Steph's delicious homemade sweets the other day, those paled in comparison. Probably she'd looked at the recipe and put her own touch on it, struggling in the kitchen. Shiro imagined it as she stared at Sora. Jibril merely closed her eyes, waiting for orders. Tearing at his hair, Sora spoke.

"......Ahhh—fine, *I'll give it a shot!*"

Elkia Royal Castle: the former royal bedchamber. Since Sora had in fact taken the one-story structure erected in the courtyard, it was now Steph's bedroom. Buried in its gigantic, literally king-size bed. Sniffling and muttering, Steph spoke.

"Liar... Didn't you say you were going to prove that Grandfather was right...?"

Steph was on her stomach, wetting the pillow she held to herself with her tears.

"Grandfather...was not a fool!"

Holding the key she carried with her everywhere, she saw her grandfather's face.

————......

Grandfather, what is this key for?

Oh, there now, Stephanie, you mustn't touch that.

Why not? What's it for?

This is the key to a place with something very important to your grandfather.

Important? Oh, I remember what Father was saying.

* * *

"Grandfather collects 'books he can't show people.'"
N-no, no, Stephanie! That is another matter!

Th-this is—the key of hope.
Hope...? What does that mean?
Ho-ho... Someday, this will be yours, Stephanie.
Really?!
Yes... But, Stephanie, listen closely to my words.

When one day you believe with all your heart that you have found a person to whom you can trust Elkia, give this to them.

——……

She'd thought back, for some reason, to events over ten years past. It had been two years since she'd received the key from her grandfather, when he'd foreseen his passing. The lock was still a mystery to her, but she never let go of the key for a minute. Why was she thinking of this now?

—Sora. The man who'd affronted her grandfather. How could she ever give it to him?

"Dora, do you have a moment?"
"Eeyaaaaaaugh!"
Vipp—Jibril appeared out of space, peering at Steph from her bedside, causing Steph to leap and scream in an excess of shock.
"Wh-wh-wha-what is it?! Y-you're trespassing!!"
"I have but a simple matter I wish to convey to you, so please don't worry about that."
Um, that wasn't exactly the point.
"It is my recommendation that you return to the library at this time."
"—What? At this time? Do you know what time—"

But, perhaps inattentive of Steph's opinion, simply bowing once and continuing unperturbed, Jibril continued.

"I came according to my own judgment that it would be better for my master. The decision is yours to make."

With this unasked-for announcement, she once more melted into space and disappeared.

…That was the Flügel for you: their thinking must have been totally different from Immanity's. Steph was disconcerted over the disjoint, but chewed over Jibril's words.

—So she was trying to tell her to go back to Sora now?

"…You must be joking; how do you expect me to go right after that!"

Steph pulled up her blanket, but the *tick-tock* of the clock in the room kept her puffy red eyes open. She thought of the words of her grandfather that she'd just remembered, and the man who'd just affronted his memory. Could it be just because Jibril came and talked to her, or was there some meaning in her having remembered that?

"…Ohh, fine, then!"

Pushing aside her blanket, Steph got up and out of bed.

◼◼◼

Elkia Grand National Library. Though Steph had been here many times before, for some reason she still entered with quiet steps. In any case, Sora and the rest were probably in the room at the back as usual. With that assumption, she slinked up to the room and found the door slightly open. Peeking in, she saw Sora, Shiro, and Jibril.

"Master, don't you think it's about time to retire?"

"Mm…just a little longer…"

But, turning the page of the book, staring unceasingly at the map, Sora answered absently. On his lap breathed Shiro, asleep, buried in pages, as Jibril pulled a blanket over her and spoke.

"I suspect that, regardless of how hard you look, it will not be possible to *defend the folly of the previous king.*"

As Jibril glanced as if aware of Steph, Steph hid with a gasp.

…It wasn't as if you could escape the notice of a Flügel just by being sneaky. But it seemed you could at least escape Sora's. Sora answered with no sign of having noticed her, and with little cheer.

"—That's not what I'm trying to do. I just noticed something *funny.*"

"Is it not the case that you…'*found* something,' for the sake of Dora?"

"I was just scouring the records for how not to conquer an animal-eared kingdom!"

Sora barked indignantly at the sly Jibril.

"Well, what do you mean by 'funny'?"

"Let's see now… There are several things."

As Jibril continued to smile with amusement, Sora answered stone-faced:

"Like I was saying this morning—*why does the Eastern Union erase players' memories?*"

That ought to deter anyone from challenging them. It was hard to see the point. At Sora's question, Jibril put her hand to her chin and thought carefully.

"Perhaps they intended to steadily build their domain *until then,* and then close themselves off."

"Yeah, that's the most obvious answer. And it's true that in the last ten years, only Elkia has challenged them."

If that was their plan, you could say they'd succeeded. But, then, why had the old king challenged them? Eight times?

"Well, you know, with the brains of Immanity, anything is possible!"

"That's what I was thinking when I was clutching my head. But it's weird."

Sora answered the smug Jibril without changing his expression.

"*Eight times*—that's not a number of times a decent person shouldering the lives of millions would attempt just out of frustration."

"—…!"

At the sign that Sora had actually been listening to her opinion, behind the door, Steph gasped quietly.

"So I researched the Eastern Union's continental domain."
Sora, pointing to the map.
"First, this here is a mine for a metal called *armatite*, right... This is the *first place the old king bet.*"
According to Jibril's books, the melting point of armatite was three thousand degrees. Such a metal was beyond the present abilities of Immanity to process—in other words, the mountain was worthless to them.
"Next, this big plain. The Eastern Union has large-scale farming here; it's a key food source for them... This is the *second place the old king bet.*"
By now, the Eastern Union had developed the land and turned it into a plain, but at the time of the game, it was a *marsh*—in other words, again, worthless.
"This coal mine was *third.* Again, it's a resource that Immanity cannot yet use. And then the fourth time, the fifth time, the sixth time...until he bet the castle the eighth time, the old king—*never bet anything that was valuable.*"
But most importantly. Sora said, pounding the map:

"Isn't all of the Eastern Union's continental domain—*originally Elkian territory?*"

—Indeed, all the territory the Eastern Union possessed on the continent was that which they had collected from the old king.
"You mean the previous king handed over to the Eastern Union all the continental resources they needed?"
"In the end, yeah. But the point is, until then, the Eastern Union had no territory on the continent, right?"
Which meant.
"The one who was trapped—was *the Eastern Union.*"
A high-tech nation with that kind of construction technology,

an advanced civilization capable of using resources with a melting point of three thousand degrees—a civilization that advanced would *need* continental resources. In this world where everything was decided by games, if even *trade* was decided by games, the tightly defensive Eastern Union would be in a tight spot.

"But what the old king kept asking for was 'one coastal city of the Eastern Union.'"

That made sense: they'd get more maritime resources, and they'd get technology. It was a reasonable condition. Except that, if it was the Eastern Union that was trapped, they should have been able to squeeze them for more. Why did he do it eight times? Holding out land worthless to Immanity, little by little.

"He had to have some reason…"

Why—did the Eastern Union erase memories when that would be a loss? Why—did Elven Gard challenge them four times? Why—… no, wait. That wasn't it.

"Why…did the old king *stop after eight times*?"

Look at it the other way. Not why did he challenge them, but why did he stop challenging them after so many times? Until the eighth time, when he bet the Royal Castle, he'd only bet things that were worthless. He could have stopped after seven times or nine. Why eight times—? Then, having thought that far, Sora reached a hypothesis.

"What if the old king—*hadn't lost his memories*?"

Taking out the map, he compared it against the data he'd gathered. Staring at the borders of several years, he whirled his thoughts around at blinding speed to confirm his flash of insight. The hypothesis was still full of holes, but it was worth looking into. The biggest holes were two. How did he *avoid having his memory erased*? And—

Meanwhile, to the furiously thinking Sora, Jibril whispered hesitantly:

"Master. You are, in theory, an Immanity."

"—Mm, huh? What's this all of a sudden?"

Sora, taken aback, stopped his train of thought and looked at Jibril.

"However, it is not the case that all Immanities think as deeply as you before they act, Master."

This was an indirect way of checking Sora as he tried to force a justification for the previous king's folly. This was the most she could say as a servant to keep him on the right path—this faint admonition from Jibril, who could never cast doubt on her lord. But Sora brushed it off.

"But *some do*. And usually no one understands them."

This time staring at the data he'd organized on the tablet, Sora.

"But to try to understand them is my *duty*."

Then he continued, as if reading the mind of Jibril, who had fallen silent.

"Jibril, it's okay if you just say it.

"This puny, powerless, abject animal—how are we supposed to believe in the humans of this world, who to you are nothing more than lower animals, both physically and mentally—that's what you want to say, right?"

"—No, I certainly didn't..."

...She certainly did. After all, no matter what kind of folly was undertaken by the previous king, what could you expect from Immanity? Jibril had decided to follow not the *lower life-form* known as Immanity, but the two *unknown entities* known as Sora and Shiro, who broke all conventional wisdom. But, at Sora's next words:

"The answer is simple—I don't believe in humans."

"What?"

Neither Jibril nor Steph, outside the room, could believe her ears.

"You probably think that, since Shiro and I are *from another world*, we're different from Immanity in this world, but it's totally the same over there. Everyone, everywhere, they're all just dumb, unbelievably crass animals—including me."

In Shiro's face as Sora deprecated himself was nothing but thick, deep despair.

—Their *old world*, covered in optical fiber, was a world shrunk to its limits, a civilization created by unbelievable wit and wisdom. Yet the massive flood of information this technology made possible, somehow only taught them more and more how foolish people could be.

"...Humans are shit. It's the same no matter what world you go to."

As Sora spit out these words, Steph clenched her key.

—She couldn't trust Sora with her grandfather's key, after all. This man...could not possibly be worthy of trust. As Steph, with these thoughts, started to move away from the door...

"But I believe in their *potential*."

...Still Sora's words held her. Jibril knelt to sit by Sora, who was tracing the floor.

"The evidence—is *here*."

Sora stroked Shiro's head as she lay in his lap, breathing softly, asleep. His sister was exhausted after stuffing such an enormous mass of information into her little head.

"If all humans were as useless as *me*, I'd have given up and hung myself long ago."

The expression of the brother now caressing his sister was not that of the man just seen in the depths of despair and disillusionment—but someone else entirely.

"In the world, *there are some...*"

These were the eyes of a gentle brother, squinting as if looking at light. They saw hope and dreams...in a pale sister, her chest minutely rising and falling.

"Some who—*because* of that puniness, that foolishness you see, come to embody learning, that special kind of divine potential, of hope, of fantasy, in a little body like that...the *real thing*."

"......"

"See, I'm a dumbass, all right." He chuckled bitterly. "I'm great at spotting 'em. The world is really full of dumbasses—sickeningly so," said Sora.

But then.

"And yet...this girl was different."

Gently passing his hand over the head on his lap, he continued.

"The day I first met Shiro—it was eight years ago."

Sora's face relaxed, as if he were thinking about something that just happened yesterday.

"This kid who was just three at the time... Can you guess what the first thing she said was when she heard my name?"

...You really are..."empty"...

—Not getting it, Jibril knit her brow. With a laugh, Sora was made to explain.

"This kid, already a polyglot at the age of three, saw the pun between my name, Sora, and me, who she could see right away was just smiling just because everyone else was, and insulted me using its double meaning—isn't that funny?"

At these words, still without shame or anger, but rather as if delirious, Sora smiled boldly and spoke.

"*My heart skipped a beat.* I was so excited—the 'real thing' really did exist."

Someone who flew beyond his petty delusions without even taking notice of them. Someone who answered when he asked, "How can you do that?" by asking back straight-faced, "How can you not?" Someone overwhelming, impossible to catch up with, who saw a different world.

"—To be the new 'big brother' of *the real thing*..."

With a strained smile, but also with resolve.

"I knew I wasn't worthy, but I *wanted to be.* I decided to believe. I thought that, no matter how worthless I was, if I tried like my life depended on it to understand, maybe I could be—maybe not like my sister, but almost.

"So, I don't believe in *humans*."
—Just as he didn't believe in himself.
"But I believe in their *potential*."
—Just as he could believe in his sister.
"The potential of humans is infinite. It's just that it's infinite *both in the positive and negative directions*."
Thus people could be infinitely wise, or infinitely foolish—and so…
"So it's like, maybe, if I'm as foolish as possible, I'll be able to catch up with my sister, who is as wise as possible?"
—Yes, just as if going in a circle. As Sora spoke bashfully, patting his little sister, Jibril, knelt beside him, watching him with deep interest.

—He probably didn't realize his negligence of the fact *he himself*, at that time, was only ten years old. At ten years old, unraveling the truth behind the words of a three-year-old child, and accepting it. And, on top of that, *respecting* it, starting to think about how to become like her. Seeing that he couldn't win with the same methods, and then immediately searching out his own path. Someone like that…who could do things like that…what would you call them? This man *who called himself dumb*—probably didn't realize.

"—I see, so *folly and genius are like two sides of a coin*—these are deep words."
Seeing Sora looking up toward the ceiling, Jibril ended up looking up herself. Squinting his eyes, through the library skylight, at the stars in the immaculate night sky, Sora told the story.
"In our old world—humans fly through the sky and even to heavenly bodies."
"—To tell the truth…I cannot believe that."
"Yeah, no one could. Not even humans ourselves."

* * *

But there were those who believed in it. There were those who believed in the dream. Looking up to the distant sky, aspiring all the more *because* they were not born with wings. In the end, people, by their own hands, built wings of steel and soared to the sky above. And then hoping higher, hoping faster, flew off the very face of planet. Because they were born with nothing, they filled themselves with ambition—and went for the other side.

—If you don't have it, you can look for it.
—If you look and it's not there, you can make it yourself.
—If you try that and you still can't get it, you look to the ends of the world.
Being born with nothing. This fact itself was the proof of the potential of *the proud, weak,* humans.
"There are some people who have *found it.* Not wannabes like me, but *the real thing,* without compare."
Not to try to understand was a crime. Because their words—were so self-evident to themselves that they could not explain.
"So it's our duty as ordinary people to try to get it."
In which case—.
"We gotta believe before we can do anything. The old king, too."
As Sora, smiling thus, dropped his gaze back to the map. Jibril simply closed her eyes, created a fantastic light from her hands, and lit Sora's work.
"What I believe is what you believe, my master and mistress. If you believe in Immanity, I shall simply follow you wherever you may go. There is nothing more."

In the back of the mind of Steph, who had been listening to the exchange as she hid outside the door. An image flashed by of the back of her grandfather, scorned as foolish, but warm and big. The back of the man, gentle and warm, who always believed in people.
—...*a person with whom you believe from your heart that you can trust Immanity...*

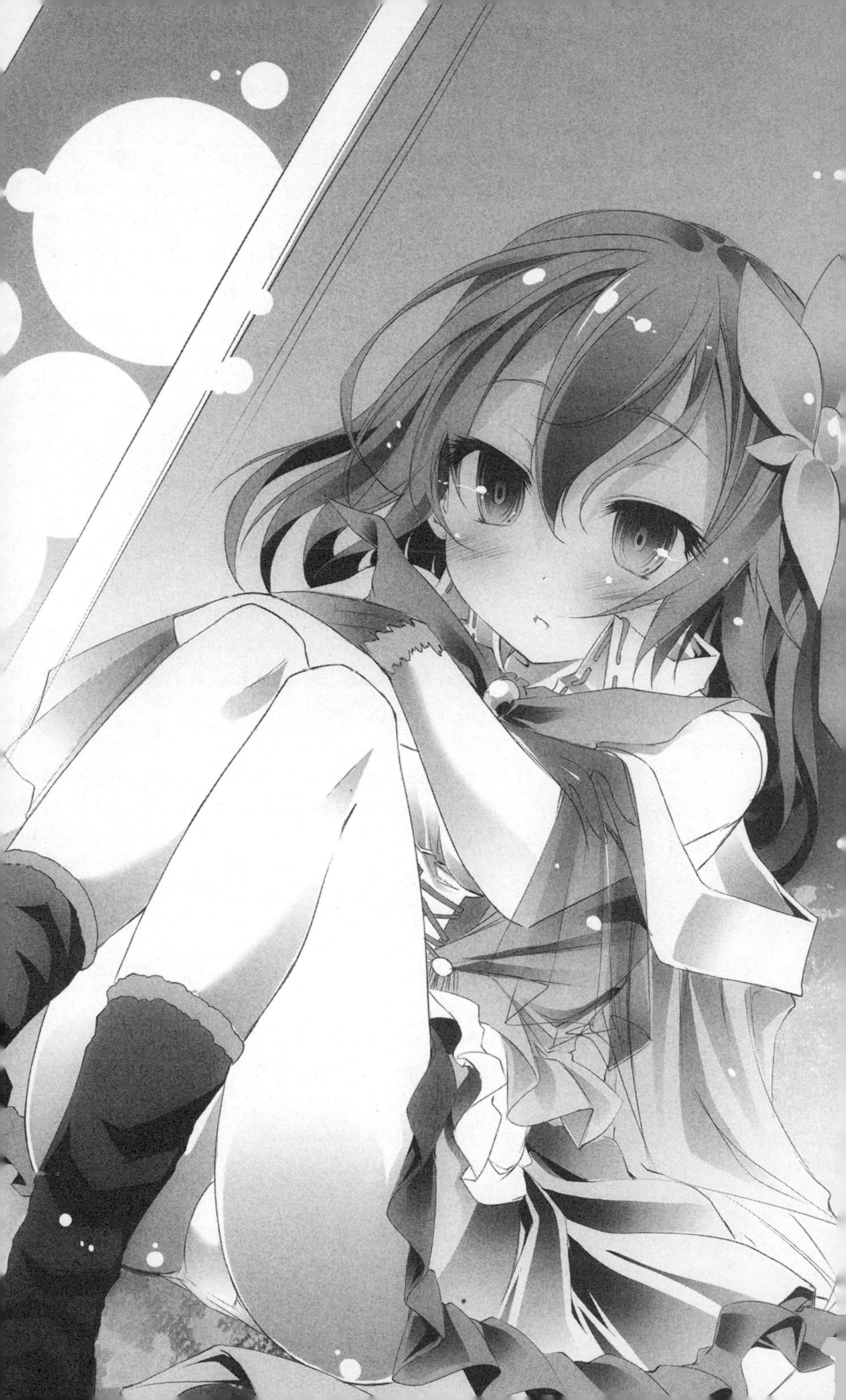

The cold, calculating man who always doubted people, so far removed from her grandfather, but, *for that very reason*. Sora, who believed in people's potential more than anyone. Might it be all right to give it to him—the key her grandfather left? Steph herself still didn't know what it meant—but. Would he...would Sora earn her grandfather's approval? Would her grandfather tell her..."You picked the right man"?

"...Sora."

Kreeek...opened the door at Steph's hand as Jibril smiled subtly and Sora looked startled. Steph simply—made up her mind, and spoke.

"I have something for you."

■ ■ ■

The next day...in the royal bedchamber that had turned into Steph's room. Steph, Sora, Shiro, and Jibril were all present.

"—So, that's the story."

The first thing that was said in reply to Steph, who'd just finished telling everything she remembered, explaining the story of the key, was this:

"No question about it, it's porn."

Steph fiercely regretted her error in selection of personnel.

"A-are you mad? How do you get that from that story?!"

"'Cos it sounded like he got nervous when you mentioned what your dad said."

"H-he said that was something different!"

"According to statistics in the *world Shiro and I come from*, 90 percent of men have a hidden stash."

"...Of R-18 stuff...adult, goods..."

"Right? Yeah, Steph, this will really come in handy. I was in fact bemoaning the lack of pr0n in this world."

Steph, out of things to say, decided to collapse on the bed quietly.

"But, Master, if you don't know where the key goes..."

"There is a 100 percent chance that the hiding place for porn is the owner's own room, i.e., here. So, no problem: in fact.

"We've *already found* a hidden room. Must be what the key's for, right?"

"...Excuse me—?"

At these words, Steph lifted her head from the bed and saw Sora and company at a distance from the bed, which she raced to close.

"First of all—I told you the bed was tilted, right? When Shiro fell."

That must have been the time a few days ago when Sora was trembling, thought Steph.

"So we backed up and looked at it carefully, and it *was* slightly tilted. So, this ornament carved into the footboard is a scale. A scale tilted left, meaning the left side is heavier, meaning there's a device on the left."

Calmly and without any sense of catharsis, Sora simply and cooly unraveled the puzzle.

"Then there's this bookcase on the left. The spaces between the shelves are slightly uneven. Even though the shelves on the right side of the room are even."

"Y-yes...n-now that you mention it."

"But, having said they're uneven, there's a pattern of just two distances, large and small."

Pointing out the shelves in order from the top.

"If we convert these into ones and zeroes we get 01, 00, 11, 10. If we look at this in binary, it's 1, 0, 3, 2. Then, if we look for books in this room that have over a thousand pages, that leaves pretty much just the encyclopedia, right?"

Drawing the encyclopedia from the shelf and opening it, Sora.

"So, the first word on page 1,032 of the encyclopedia is *lighthouse*, in Immanity. Well, if we're going to interpret something here as a 'lighthouse,' it's got to be some lighting fixture like a candlestick or a chandelier or something."

Clomping over to a candlestick by the wall of the room, Sora went on:

"Also, the word had, at the center, a depressed line, as if made with a pen without ink."

Steph and Jibril looked.

—Indeed, there was a faint depression.

"Which means it's the candlestick at the *center* of the left side of the room. Plus, there are three arrows to the left of the word to indicate an idiom, so—"

He tilted the candlestick, left, three times.

"Finally, to the right, there's an arrow referring to the related entry *harbor* on page 605. Which means—"

He tilted the candlestick right once. Then the candlestick came off...

—Revealing four dials inside.

"Now after this is what Shiro solved, so I'll hand it off."

They slapped their hands together, and Shiro turned the dials.

"Factorize...the number of times...the lines cross...in *lighthouse* and *harbor*...in the Immanity writing system."

There was a click.

"...Ex-actly...four digits...result: *2642*..."

Sora spoke to Steph and Jibril as they watched in a daze. As if showing a swift magic trick, he clapped his hands to get things moving again.

"Right, right—and then, what do you know! Look, behind the curtain, one block in the wall is sticking out oddly!... Oh, ya know, this is kind of tough; last time Shiro and I just barely managed to shove it together to open it; it probably hasn't been maintained. Jibril, give us a hand."

"Oh, yes—at your command."

Jibril did so with a light push.

"And then, the moment you've been waiting for—"

* * *

Grmmmmm.

"The bookcase moves..."

And, after it finished moving, beyond—

"And here is our locked door. This must be where your key goes, right?"

Sora played with the key in his hand he'd received from Steph, utterly carefree.

"—..."

Yes, all too carefree. All too easygoing. The trick that the previous king had probably racked his brains to prepare—had been solved so nonchalantly that even Jibril was left speechless while Steph shouted:

"Wh-wh-when did you figure this out?!"

"I thought I already said—*the day Shiro fell from the bed.*"

Shiro nodded.

—"Wait, wait. Hold on," said Steph. "...You refer to the day I was made into a dog and you played against Jibril?"

"Yeah, good memory."

"I couldn't forget that trauma even if I wanted to! But anyhow—!"

—That day, first thing in the morning, Steph had found Sora shaking. They'd played blackjack, and Steph had lost. And then they'd gone out to meet the nobles—and then to the library.

"When did you have time to find this—?!"

"When you got called out about the nobles, there was about an hour before you came back, right?"

He was saying casually that he'd *solved this contrivance in an hour,* while simply killing time—a puzzle over which Steph had brooded forever. Though Steph gaped, still, apparently unaware of just what he and his sister had done, Sora continued.

"But, yeah, last time we got stuck because we couldn't find the key."

"B-but, Master, a door like that—"

"Yeah, we could have even just picked the lock, but what fun is a *puzzle-solving game* if you cheat?"

Sora smiling, Shiro nodding. Yes, it was *just a game*...

And then, softening his expression, going, *eh-heh, eh-heh.*

"Sooo, shall we proceed to view these treasure texts he went so far to hide—oh, I'll cover Shiro's eyes."

"...Mmg...not fair..."

"Time is unfair in a fair way. Just wait seven more years."

"I'm telling you, it's not porn!"

Sora placed the key he'd received from Steph in the keyhole and turned it. The door opened with the groan of high-quality metal fittings.

——......Sora, though he'd just been charging under the assumption it was porn—along with everyone else, all present, somehow—was struck dumb.

Inside was a windowless library. A dust-covered study, with wooden shelves buried in books, ornaments with a tasteful air, a desk, a chair. But, contrasting to its peace, everyone must have felt the certain *dread*. It told them this wasn't a place into which to step lightly, and it held back their feet. With a gulp, Sora slowly went through the doorway of the study. His gaze came to rest upon the book that lay open on the study table in the center, stroking just once the surface of a page rendered illegible by dust. The writing that appeared was bold, and it said just one thing.

To the monarch not of Immanity's last days—but of its resurgence, we leave this.

Sora carefully turned the page, and it continued.

As king, we are not the Wise.

Rather we shall most likely be known as a rare Fool. Still, we take up our pen for the sake of the monarch of resurgence, not us. In faith that our shallow and desperate struggles may serve the monarch to come.

"......"

Peering at Sora, standing at a loss for words, Shiro and Jibril understood and felt at a loss themselves.

—What was there was everything. Over the span of countless matches with other nations in the life of the so-called fool king. Including all eight matches with the Eastern Union. The substance of this man who had charged headily, lost unceremoniously, and *dedicated himself to exposing their hand*—all of it.

—Knowing that, at the rate things were going, the human race would extinguish itself soon, and that his actions would only hasten this. But he'd taken the offensive anyway, under the assumption of defeat. That was the part he played, the fool, dedicated to exposing the cards of the Eastern Union and *all his enemies*, while scorned as the rarest of fool kings. All the memories he had managed to grasp as a mere human—.

—It must have been.

"The old king...*didn't lose his memories*."

"But—how!"

Jibril, wondering how he could have escaped the Eastern Union's memory erasure she hadn't been able to escape herself. But Sora had an idea. Just a guess—but close to a conviction.

"Jibril. A fool with money walks into a casino. What do you do to empty him out?"

"—Make him look like there's a game he can win, and get him to attack...many...times..."

Jibril opened her eyes as if she'd seen it.

"The old king was *probing them*. Eight times. Intentionally giving them worthless land—and then, to take it back."

But even if they didn't erase his memory, there was no way the Eastern Union could allow him to talk. Therefore, probably—.

"Maybe he said he wouldn't tell anyone his whole life..."

But that—*didn't cover after death*... That was it. For humans, unable to use magic like the Elves, to grasp and remember the nature of the memory-erasing game was the only chance they had.

* * *

"—'Let the next king be the greatest gambler among humans'...eh."

"......Yeah."

Sora whispered the will of the late king with feeling, and Shiro understood the meaning and took in a breath herself. He—must have known. Aware of the flaw in the tournament to decide the monarch, that other countries could interfere, he had ordered it anyway. What he sought—was gamers who could get past it, while still only human, to take the crown. For *only one who could break through foreign interference head-on would be able to make use of these records.* For these were records that made very clear at length his conclusion that they could never win fighting fair.

"...Steph."

"Wh-what is it?"

To Steph, uncomprehending, perhaps, of the situation, starting at Sora's serious face.

"...Your grandfather...no, the *previous king*...he was really *your grandfather.*"

Remembering Steph, who'd even bet her panties to reveal their hand.

He'd been reviled as a fool, by his people, by the world. And he'd went on playing the fool, dedicating himself to revealing his enemies' hand. What kind of heart had such resolve? To keep believing in the "monarch of resurgence"—such *faith in Immanity.* He had gambled on the chance that, from the humans at the very bottom of the ranks, someone would appear who could rout the other races. On that infinitely small but nonzero chance, he had placed his faith and bet his honor, his name, his pride...his own life.

A life of shame and failure piled up high to set the stage for one invincible blow. The two-in-one "monarch of resurgence" with whom that blow was entrusted could only stand and stare. Sora looked down at his shirt which read "I ♥ PPL" and simply said:

"See, Jibril, there are some like that—what do you think: *pretty sick*, huh?"

"…You…may be right."

With the sense that she'd caught a glimpse of that in which her master believed, Jibril, intending to revise her understanding, closed her eyes and nodded. Sora, taking out his phone, started his task scheduler.

What he slid his finger to input was, indeed, without hesitation, this one phrase.

—*Objective: Swallow up the Eastern Union.*

⏻ CHAPTER 4
CHECKMATE

The embassy—no, once Elkia's castle, now the "Empire State Building." As she looked up from below, Shiro had one comment.

"...My neck hurts."

"Jeez, why does it have to be this big... Wait, Immanity doesn't have this kind of construction technology, does it?"

To Sora, complaining as he held his neck, Jibril replied indifferently.

"That goes without saying. The Eastern Union remodeled the building any number of times after they took it."

Hmm... Sora answered, "...Well, I was already pretty sure...but, yeah, I think we're gonna have to just charge into this baby."

"...? What are you talking about?—And, wait—"

Steph, with a tinge of irritation, pointed to the ground.

"May I finally ask *what we are doing here*?"

—And likewise Shiro and Jibril, having also been led here with no explanation, looked to Sora as if agreeing with Steph's words.

"Soft, soft, I come but to lay my eyes upon the fair 'animal girls.'"

Sora dodged the question and marched ahead.

"H—wait a minute, this may be within Elkia's borders, but it's an embassy, you know!" protested Steph.

"I'm aware. And it *was* our castle."

"Ngh, no, I-I mean—i-it's a violation of sovereignty!"

"Who said anything about violating anyone's sovereignty? We have an appointment."

"Wha? That's—"

Impossible, Steph was going to say before she was interrupted.

"Right—Gramps?"

Just as Sora said this…

…The door of the giant building opened to reveal a figure.

"—Welcome, King Sora and Queen Shiro of Elkia."

A gray-haired, wolf-eared, bushy-tailed, *hakama*-wearing Were-beast descended the steps of the entrance to the height of four people or so and bowed deeply.

"It is a pleasure to make your acquaintance. I am the deputy ambassador of the Eastern Union in Elkia—my name is Ino Hatsuse."

Thus deferentially spoke the old man—Ino Hatsuse.

"Uh, what? H-how did you make contact?!"

Sora didn't know what Steph was getting all that excited about, but he answered:

"Well, you know, this morning, this guy was *looking at me while I was on the library balcony.*"

—Huh?

"So then I signaled, 'I'll be over in a minute,' and Gramps nodded back. See, we have an appointment."

"…Um, no, that does not make sense," protested Steph.

"H—wait a minute. It's thirty kilometers from here to that library!"

"You're right. It really surprised me to see how good Werebeast eyes are."

—No. That wasn't the point. If we were talking about Werebeasts, then fine. But the question was. How did *Sora* see that? But without addressing that in the slightest. Ino responded calmly as if the details were already known.

"It is my understanding you have business with the ambassador of the Eastern Union in Elkia—Izuna Hatsuse."

Thus—Ino anticipated their business. Ino's narrowed eyes, the *mind-reading eyes of the Werebeast*, faced them all.

Steph's breath was stolen for a moment. They were—yes, just like Sora's, no, even more. Eyes that seemed to see through everything, to peer into her head—

"I'm glad we could get straight to it. So, let's go; show me the way."

But, from Sora, who stood as if utterly unaffected by these eyes, taking them face-on, what did Ino glean?

"—Come right this way, please."

As all he did was to invite them inside.

■■■

Entering, going through the lobby, boarding the elevator. From among buttons that went up to 80, he pressed 60, and the elevator began to rise.

"Uh?! Wh-what is this; the floor is moving?!"

Ignoring the lone bewildered Steph, Ino said:

"I must say, though, we would appreciate it if next time you made your visit according to the official procedures."

To his words, which implied, *and not some stunt like that*, it was Steph who surprisingly enough reacted.

"Some talk. Has the Eastern Union ever responded to the official procedures?!"

As if genuinely taken aback by Steph's sarcastic words, Ino peered into Steph's eyes and spoke.

"—What, you have in fact posted...?"

At Ino, seeming to read Steph's thoughts to see that she was telling a startling truth, Steph flinched for a moment at those eyes that read her soul, but stubbornly stood her ground.

"O-of course we have! Since the reign of my grandfather, we have sent any number of letters regarding trade and diplomacy, and not once have we received a reply. How dare you feign ignorance!"

"...I deeply apologize. Next time, please address your inquiries directly to me, Ino Hatsuse."

With that, Ino sighed and put a hand to his forehead.

"As you know, since *that incident*, there are a remarkable number among us who hold an excess of hostility toward Elkia... Since the last game with your previous king, I have not heard once of a letter..."

"Wha—! You li—"

"I suspect that your letters have been disposed of within the lower ranks. There is no excuse for this; I will identify those who ordered and carried out this grave discourtesy and see to it that they are punished severely. I beg your forgiveness."

Ino's finished words, cutting off the doubting Steph, shut her up, bringing to her face rage and shame.

—It appeared that he really hadn't known.

"Quite the 'great country'; but I suppose it's all one can expect from Werebeasts."

At Jibril's snide quip, Ino's gaze sharpened subtly.

"Wait, Steph, what's *'that incident'*?"

Sora seemed to suppose that because letters were not arriving no appointment could be made.

"...It involves the reconstruction after our castle was taken."

Sighing with a sense of pain, Steph explained.

"Elkia built a new castle from the standpoint that having an embassy grander than our castle would affect our dignity as a nation."

"Hmm, the castle we have now, right?"

"In response, the Eastern Union undertook a large-scale remodel, and then again, as if to rub our noses in it... Elkia is no match for the Eastern Union when it comes to construction technology either, so, well, you know, things happened."

"Oh, yeah, I hate those events; they really get on my nerves..." Sora muttered.

To this, Jibril took the opportunity for another jab. "It's all the more irritating for the tendency of Werebeast, at Rank Fourteen, to look down inordinately at Immanity, at Rank Sixteen.—I seem to recall reading a certain phrase in one of my master's books."

With a smile of recognition, Jibril said:

"—'The pot calling the kettle black.'"

Hah-hah-hah, Ino laughed, and he answered:

"How very apt; I cannot agree more. And, to be told this by Rank Six, how it smarts."

But, continued Ino:

"In that case, your old curios floating around in the sky under a pile of books constitute the *pot*, I presume?"

"Hee-hee; there's no need to overexert yourself; you're welcome to speak your true meaning as plainly as you like," Jibril answered, with neither breaking a crack in their smiles.

"That is, *in rank, life span, physical abilities, knowledge, wisdom... in everything we are inferior to you, O Flügel, but as wretched, inadequate creatures crawling the earth, please allow us the luxury of looking down on one of the few life-forms we can find below us!*"

"Hah-hah-hah, I should not expect to hear such a novel viewpoint but from a defective product such as yourself who travels in the company of these *hairless monkeys*."

"Why, yes, for narrow-minded mongrels such as yourself, it certainly must be an eye opener!"

"Hah-hah-hah!"

"Tee-hee-hee!"

"...Hey, Steph."

"...Not that I can't guess, but what is it?"

"Is it just me, or is there way too much tension in this world? Also, by *hairless monkeys*, does he mean us?"

"In a world that was fighting for almost an eternity, when you ban combat out of the blue, some grudges would have to remain…"

To say nothing of the fact that—

"…They're the two most bloodthirsty races amongst all the Ixseeds."

As for the second question—Steph shook her head to indicate that no response was necessary.

"Hee-hee-hee, I'm sure your children can sleep better at night now that violence is forbidden."

"Hah-hah-hah, perhaps they do, unlike some with no skills besides killing, who have gone and settled into retirement."

……——.

The two siblings, Sora and Shiro, both thought the same thing: No wonder violence was forbidden in this world.

■■■

Escaping from the almost crackling air of the elevator, on the sixtieth floor where they arrived, Steph seemed already exhausted, and once they were led to a space that suggested a reception chamber, she sat down immediately.

"S-so tiring…"

Though he sympathized completely, Sora only looked around.

"…If you'll excuse me, I shall call Izuna Hatsuse and return in a bit."

Having watched Ino take a bow and retreat beyond view. Sora started taking in their surroundings, and Steph took his lead to look around the room.

"…But one must say it is magnificent. The difference between our civilizations is all too palpable," she said.

A room made of marble and some other materials that one could tell at a glance were rare. Inside the leather sofa were even springs. But such things were not what Sora was looking for.

"By the way, Master, how did you contact Werebeast?"

"…Jibril, have you noticed no one's brought it up? Take a hint."

"I apologize; unlike the mind-reading Werebeast, I could not help but wonder."

Sora knew that Jibril with the *unknown* before her eyes equaled a horse with a *carrot* dangling before it.

"……Whoop."

Sora, putting his index finger to his lips, brought out his phone. A video he'd apparently recorded using optical zoom and also applying an upscaling app to capture at the maximum magnification. In it was just barely visible an outline resembling an old man's.

—So, in other words. Sora actually *hadn't really seen Ino*. It just so happened that a figure who seemed to be looking at him happened into his lens. He'd only gestured on the assumption that the person probably saw him. In short—it was just a bluff.

Jibril's intrigue was obvious. However— (What purpose would such a bluff serve against *Werebeast, who can read thoughts*?) she seemed to think. It didn't appear that Ino had known that the letters weren't arriving, either—. While Jibril ruminated thus…

"…Brother, look."

"Yeah, I know."

Another question rained upon her.

"…Master, do you *know* this?"

Jibril pointed to it—. A TV. Yes, it was exactly what Sora had been looking for. The shape was significantly different from what Sora knew, but there was no way around it—it was a TV.

"—Hmm, now I know for sure…"

"What do you know?"

But he answered with a sly grin.

"I'll tell you later. Werebeasts have good ears. I'm sure they're listening already—right, Gramps?"

"—Please forgive the wait."

Ino, clicking the door open and coming back in.

"This is the ambassador of the Eastern Union in Elkia—Izuna Hatsuse."

With this introduction, what came through the doorway…

…had black eyes and black hair in a bob, a tail and long animal ears, big as those of a fennec fox, along with traditional Japanese-style garb tied at the waist with a big ribbon—and, however you looked at it, her age couldn't have been out of single digits.

"Cu—"
Though Steph almost forgot her position and said *cute*, before she could get the words out…

"King Crimson!"

"Ee-hee-hee beautiful little girl with animal ears why don't you come play with big brother I'm certainly no one suspicious…"
"…Boink, boink…poof, poof…fluffy fluffy…hee-hee-hee-hee-hee…"
—When did they move? Sora and Shiro, whom even Jibril's eyes couldn't catch, were already well on their way, precisely petting the girl's head and tail. To these two, the Werebeast girl—Izuna—responded with a cute, innocent voice.

"Who said you assholes could touch me, please."

…—.
"—Huh?"
"…Minus, fifty…cuteness…points."
The siblings each mumbled their reactions and took a big step back. But.
"Who said you could stop, please."
"Uh…um, what?"
"Get the hell on with it, please."
Izuna was like a cat that wanted to be petted, squinting her eyes, stretching out her neck.
"Uhh, oh, it's all right?"

"Dumbass, of course it's all right, please. You just touched me without any goddamn warning, please."

While her manner and expression failed to match, somehow Sora seemed to catch on.

"...Oh. Don't think putting 'please' at the end of any goddamn sentence makes it polite, please!"

"...?! It doesn't, please?!"

Come to think of it. In this world, you couldn't do anything to people they didn't want you to. So, when they were able to pet Izuna, it meant that she permitted it.

"Please don't mind my granddaughter. She has only been in Elkia for one year and is not yet skilled in the Immanity tongue—and, also."

With that, Ino swiftly changed his expression.

"You damn hairless monkeys! Just 'cos I've gone to the trouble of bowing my head for your scrawny asses you better not get cocky you little shits what makes you think you can get your filthy hands all over my lovely little granddaughter you're good as dead—"

—And, with that, restored his polite smile.

"—is an example of the type of conversation I must caution you to avoid."

Sora responded with half-closed eyes and a soft remark.

"—Gramps, this has nothing to do with the Immanity tongue and everything to do with you."

"I'm afraid your meaning eludes me, sir."

In Sora's shadow, Shiro spoke, glaring at Ino.

"...I hate this old fart... Minus a thousand points."

And, as Izuna gave the impression of wanting to be petted, Shiro fluffed her and said:

"...But Iz-zy...so cute with that...potty mouth...plus ten points."

As Shiro petted and fluffed her, Ino, visibly suppressing rage, spoke quietly.

"—Izuna. If you don't like it, you can tell them."

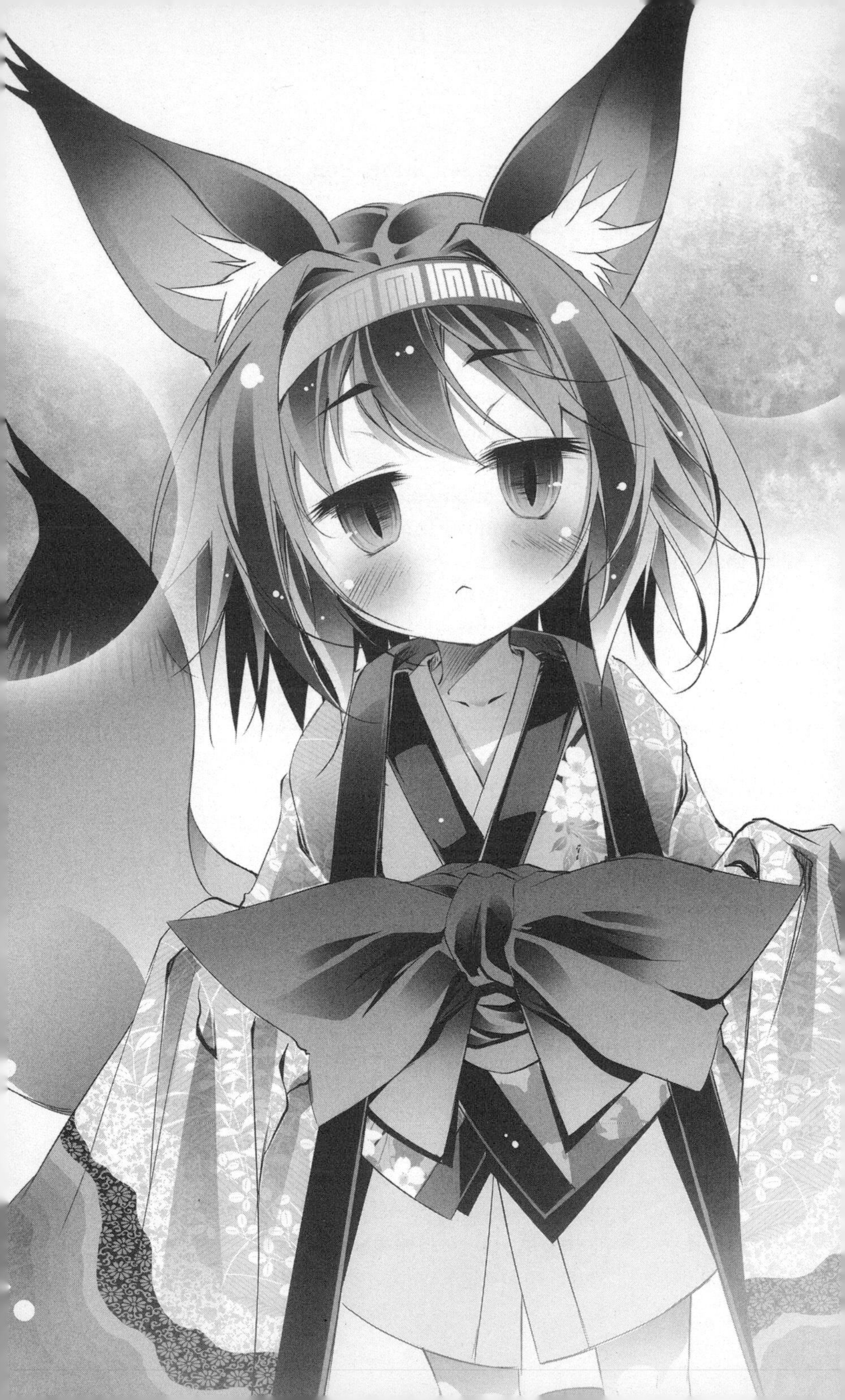

"I like it just fine, please. It feels good, so keep doing it, bitch, please."

"Oh, then me, too."

Fluff fluff fluff fluff...

"You're pretty good for goddamn hairless monkeys, please. Do it more, please."

To Izuna, expressionless as a cat, yet closing her eyes as she spoke, Sora.

"In that case, can you stop calling us hairless monkeys?"

"Why the hell should I do that, please?"

"Because we'd be happier if you called us by our names. I'm Sora. This is my sister, Shiro. Nice to meet you."

"...Nice to meet you..."

"Understood, please. Nice to meet ya, please. Sora, Shiro."

Fluff fluff fluff...

"—Gah, you won't let your grampy touch you, but you'll let the hairless monkeys, Izuna!"

"Grampy...you suck; your claws hurt, please."

Sora laughed at Ino, who looked depressed at Izuna's instant answer.

"*Heh-heh-heh...* My sister is a master of *Nintendogs*, and I am a master of the touch-based erotic video game. For us, pinpoint adjustments of our touch based on her reactions is but a trifle. You better respect the hand-eye coordination of the gamer, old man."

"...Not that...we have any...experience...with the real thing."

"Why you gotta kill it like that, huh?!"

■■■

Sitting on the sofa, looking at the ceiling with an expression of rapture, Izuna, and, tense at the temples, Ino. On the other side of the table, Sora and Shiro, making four, sitting across from each other.

"Well, then, may I inquire as to why you *monkey bastards* are here?"

"You can read my thoughts, right? Why do I have to say anything?"

"This is a place of diplomacy, a place where words are exchanged orally or in writing; or is that too challenging for a monkey to understand?"

"…Just because we're better with your granddaughter than you are, old man, you don't gotta get all pissy. Jeez."

As Ino's smile cracked, Jibril continued, beaming.

"Master, inadequacy is a central part of the soul of the Werebeast, as fragile as glasswork. Perhaps you might refrain from upsetting him unnecessarily. It is most pitiful."

Ino, his smile on the brink of finally breaking and making up his mind that he should just blissfully forget everything and kick these asses out, peered into Sora's eyes.

—That instant, an unexpected chill ran down Ino's spine.

What was there was not the silly wag who'd sat there just a moment ago. What was there was a man full of confidence verging on arrogance, a mind in the midst of ungodly calculation, and unmistakably—the *king of a race.*

"My demand is simple, Ino Hatsuse."

Sora flashed a cheeky grin with this, and then said with a serious mien:

"Give me your granddaughter's panties. I'll give you Steph's."

"—Excuse me?!"

"Hey, monkey bastard, there's a goddamn line you might not wanna cross!"

Steph, tossed abruptly into the fire, and Ino shouted at the same time. But, as if it surprised him, Sora replied:

"What, you don't want Steph's? You'd prefer Jibril's?"

"I have no qualms, be it the command of my master."

Just as Sora spoke, Jibril started peeling down her panties. Ino face-palmed, squeezing out his voice as if trying to hold something back.

"Hey, monkey. If you're just here to be an asshole, get the—"

"Wha, you can't have Shiro's; to desire an eleven-year-old's panties, there's something wrong with you, Gramps. Or—y-you wanted mine?! Uhh, wait, that's... I mean, I'm a tolerant guy, but that does kinda gross me out..."

To Ino, finally starting to lose it, still Sora.

"Come on, Gramps, are you sure? I'm saying I'd *make a deal* just for Izuna's panties!"

"Look, you son of a bitch—*if you're not going to say what you're really here for*, then get the—"

As Ino held his forehead as if he was getting a headache.

—Sora, like a gambler who'd just made the haul of a century. Beaming ironically.

"—Gramps, I hate to say it, but we know you're just *pretending to read minds.*"

Bip. From Ino came a reaction the human eye could scarcely detect, but more than enough for Sora.

"*If you're not going to say what you're really here for*... Huh. That's pretty good; it does make it sound like you're reading my mind, but, if you could really read my mind, you'd have accepted a game for panties. 'Cos it wouldn't really be about the stupid panties; it would be about the side effect, i.e.—

"You'd never overlook the importance of *erasing my memories that tell everything about the Eastern Union's games.*"

To Sora's words and insinuating smirk...

"......"

...Ino had no response but to stay expressionless. After all—. Yes, Sora's pupils, heartbeat, even the sound of his blood flow. Every little thing told that the man here spoke *with absolute conviction.*

"So, now that that's *confirmed*, shall I get to your request and *say what I'm really here for?*"

Sora crossed his legs and adjusted his posture.

"In the names of the agent plenipotentiary of the kingdom of Elkia, last nation of Rank Sixteen, Immanity: Sora and Shiro."

Taking Shiro's hand, lifting it as if in oath, Sora.

"Your fine nation, the Eastern Union, of Rank Fourteen, the Werebeasts, has been chosen as the first sacrifice in our path of glorious global conquest, and for this we *celebrate*. Now, in a *battle of nations*, we demand—"

With a smile of blatant hostility, he announced transcendently:

"—*everything on the continent you bitches have.*"

—At these words, everyone's eyes, except Sora's and Shiro's, opened wide. Even Ino, and even Izuna, who had been spacing out until then, changed their countenance. It was just—too unhinged a demand.

"Oh, and what we're betting is still Steph's panties, FYI."

"Ex-excuse me?!"

"Too bad you didn't shake on Izzy's panties while you had the chance, Grandpa."

The wagers were all the territory the Eastern Union had on the continent—and Stephanie Dola's panties? As even Jibril began to wonder about the mental soundness of the man before them, Sora continued with completely unwavering confidence.

"Sorry, Gramps—it's *check*."

While all sat at a loss as to the meaning of his words, perhaps having the most courage, or perhaps out of obedience to her curiosity, Jibril asked:

"Ma-Master, ehm, what do you mean?"

"Huh? You still don't get it?"

"…Oh…" said Shiro, coming out of deep thought.

"That's my Shiro; you got it, right? Yeah—so this means the Eastern Union is trapped."

But, as still no one but Sora and Shiro seemed to grasp the meaning of his words, Sora spoke listlessly.

"Mm, okay, I'll explain for you all, including this *self-professed* mind-reading grampa.

"The Eastern Union, half a century back, rapidly developed a high level of technology... But it can be tough to be an advanced civilization."

Settling deep into the sofa—the nice, springy sofa, Sora continued.

"The TV in this room, the elevator back there, this sofa... all this modern technology isn't possible without continental resources. They're their lifeline, no kidding. But the Eastern Union started as an island nation. They had to get their hands on those continental resources any way they could—but, *before that*, Elven Gard challenged them.

"What a pickle! The only trick they had was taking challenges, but, then, if they beat the greatest country in the world, then no one would take on their *mysterious unbeatable game*, and they wouldn't get the continent. But they couldn't lose—why is this?"

With a broad grin, Sora put up a finger.

"Now, let's unravel the puzzle step by step. *Question one:* Why did they need to erase memories of an unbeatable game?"

Shiro answered this question.

"...Because...*if they didn't...it wouldn't be unbeatable*...anymore."

Why would the Eastern Union incorporate a demand that contradicted their strategy of taking challenges? It must have been because, despite its downside, *they had to*. If they intentionally lost to Elven Gard, then their game would be revealed—and then it would cease to be unbeatable.

"But there's still a hole, even then."

To erase all memories of the game certainly seemed the best possible way to make it impossible to counter. And yet...

* * *

"Even if you erase their memories—you can't erase the result that they *lost*."

Jibril gasped, while Ino remained expressionless.

"Now let's move on. *Question two:* Why did Elven Gard step up *four times*?"

"...After losing...they tried to break down...the unbeatable game... *from the results*?"

Indeed—Unlike Elkia, Elven Gard was a vast country. To brace themselves for a few losses in scouting was but a small matter for them.

"After losing once, Elven Gard must have guessed that it was a game where you couldn't use magic. For Elves to lose, you know, that's pretty much the first thing one would think of."

Raising a finger, Sora continued.

"Still not knowing what the game was, with their memories erased—but knowing that it must be a game that annulled magic— the second time, they got someone outside to cast magic while they played. But *then they lost anyway*. And so, the third time, they probably somehow uncovered the nature of the game."

Man, if only I could use some crazy official cheat like magic, noted Sora.

"And so they went in for the long-awaited fourth time—*but they lost*. Am I right, Gramps?"

"......You certainly have an impressive imagination."

Ino responded as though Sora's guess was nothing more than just that. Yet thinking he could beat Sora in a battle of bluffs—that was the greatest blunder. Picking up on the faint waver in his expression, Sora smiled and held up two fingers.

"But this raises two issues. First, why did Elven Gard lose? And then this is the big one—*why didn't they try again*?"

—Indeed. The question wasn't why they tried. It was *why they stopped trying.* This was a piece of information too big to overlook in a game where the simple result of having lost told everything.

"There are two possibilities. One is that they realized that the game was theoretically impossible to win."

Then lowering one of his fingers.

"The other—that *they figured out the game, but they couldn't figure out why they lost.*"

With a laugh and a confident smile, Sora said:

"—But, in the first case, they'd win if they uncovered it. Which means it must be the second."

Jibril, of Rank Six, Flügel, felt a chill of awe down her spine. Sora's reasoning was supported and supplemented by all the fragments of information that Jibril knew. Such extraordinary, even godlike powers of reasoning—.

"But that makes things confusing. A *game that can be understood without understanding why you lost?*"

Sora, grinning drily, as if to say *that's so weird, how could that be?*

"And we just got the key to unlocking this mystery from you, Gramps."

Into Ino's eyes. The eyes of Werebeast, who claimed to read minds, Sora peered with an ironic smile.

"*Question three:* Why would you *lie* that you can read minds?"

"*...Because they can't...*"

Nodding to Shiro's immediate answer, Sora.

"And they must have to lie because that implies something they can't let anyone know, right?

"Are you starting to see it yet? *Question four:* What kind of game *looks like you can win in theory but actually makes you lose?*"

Sora, apparently having fun.

"—Now, here's a hint!"

With theatrical gesture as if enjoying telling a riddle, Sora continued.
"Flügel, Elf, Immanity. It makes all these races of entirely different characteristics lose every time, it can only be used in defense,
it requires erasing opponents' memories, it's good for a race with
superior technology who can't read minds—what is it?!"
With a glance toward the TV, Shiro answered.

"...A video game...with all cheats enabled..."

It appeared that neither Steph nor Jibril understood the answer.
That was no surprise: The Eastern Union must be the only country
in the world that knew the concept of *video games*. This was why—
they had to erase memories to conceal them. This was why they
could never lose.   ·
—Using video games, with them as the game masters, they could
cheat all they wanted, do whatever they wanted, and there was no
way—
—*anyone* would know.

"This makes even magic pointless... Well, well, now *that's* a tech
nation; not bad, eh?"
In these words from Sora was not the sound of irony, but that of
genuine praise.
"All that big talk about reading minds was to give 'em something
to quell the question they'd be left with as the result of losing—*Why
did we lose?*—so they wouldn't come searching. All you guys can do
is to *tell when someone's lying*—you can't *read minds*."
Yes—it was exactly the same as what Sora was good at. Seeing
through expressions, gestures, voices to the lies behind them. They
just were able to use their outrageous senses to incorporate heart-
beats, blood flow. It was exactly the same, logically, as how a talented
fraudster would pass themselves off as a *spiritualist*.

"......"
—Bull's-eye. Ino, struck dead on, had no words. However, without

showing it on his face, he was being eaten away by doubts. Until Sora first realized they couldn't read minds—that is, even during all that crap talk about Izuna's panties and such—Sora had showed no reaction of unease whatsoever. It seemed it could only be that he had *eliminated from the start* the risk that his mind would be read. But, to those thoughts and, ironically enough, as if reading his mind, Sora answered:

"Ain't it weird, Gramps? I never showed *any reaction to your bluff* from the beginning."

Erk, Ino's expression almost went, or did it? As this alone filled Ino's mind, Sora continued snidely.

"Yes. I knew you guys couldn't read minds—*from the beginning.* How could this be?"

And now, for the final question—went Sora.

"*Question five:* Why did our previous king lose to you as many as *eight times?*"

Shiro, Steph, and Jibril knew the answer to this question. Therefore—

"This question—is for you, you hairy old shit. You gotta have some idea."

"—...!"

—*Their* previous king? He was the only one who'd played the Eastern Union without having his memory erased, when they took their continental domain from him. But they played on the condition that he wouldn't tell anyone; how could—

—Wait, *no*. It wasn't that; it was—! As if waiting for Ino's thoughts to reach *that*, Sora grinned, and then spoke.

"Yeah, you got it, huh? The fact that the previous king *was able to tell us all about it* is the proof that you couldn't read his intention—you couldn't read his thoughts."

Which were—.

"—That his covenant not to tell anyone his whole life—*didn't cover after he died.*"

As Ino tried to hold up his mask of calm, he could feel his blood draining. Were that the case—. It would mean that this man, truly—knew everything about their games. If it were exposed, the Eastern Union would be——.

"So, you get the picture now, Gramps?"

Grinning ear to ear and continuing idly.

"Now you're in a tough spot, huh? You have to erase my memory somehow. But if you play me betting your continental domain just for Steph's panties, you'll *basically be admitting I'm right*."

Yes—and so. The move Ino should make was a given. In this situation—

"*You're gonna dismiss everything I've said as crazy rambling*— that's your only choice, to turn down the game and run."

Sora intercepted Ino's thoughts mercilessly, like a hunter giddily cornering his prey.

—And said: "Did you think I'd leave you an avenue of escape?"

"We bet *all of Immanity*—the Race Piece."

The moment Sora said it, before his eyes materialized a game piece, shining softly, as if made of light. Yes, it was…what, in this world where even the God was decided by games, was required to challenge the God—one of sixteen pieces to collect, by conquest of all the races.

—The Immanity Piece. The piece of Immanity—was the king.

—No one there had beheld it. Even Jibril, who had lived for six thousand years, was seeing a Race Piece with her own eyes for the first time. This made sense. For, in all the games played in the ages since the Ten Covenants. No one had ever bet a Race Piece, for it meant to *wager all the rights of the race*. In the event of a loss, it was tantamount to consigning the race to enslavement for eternity. In other words, it meant—*the end*.

* * *

"A-are you in—*gmph*?!"

Steph, who seemed to have finally grasped the situation, was about to scream, "Are you insane?" when Jibril deftly grabbed her by the mouth.

—With this, a wager was made of the piece of a race in one more struggle for continental territory.

"With this, you'll *also* tell the world I'm right if you run!"

Thus, with a smile, Sora looked into the eyes of a Werebeast who claimed to read minds—

"Look, it's check again—no, now it's *checkmate*."

—showing Ino no trace of fear, and spoke without humility.

"—Did you see this coming, Gramps?"

As Sora grinned, a line of sweat fell from Ino's brow.

—What was this? For the lowest of races, a race down to its last city, about to bet their Race Piece and lose everything, to *initiate* a challenge against the Eastern Union, which had an unbeatable game, and on top of that to seize the upper hand, *cornering them logically*—what was going on?

But—Ino, just barely regaining his composure—no, *feigning* it— answered:

"I can only applaud your remarkable *imagination*. However, King Sora, isn't there something you've overlooked?"

Ino struck back at the desperation in his heart with his one unshakable fact.

"Even assuming this *fantasy* of yours is true—would that not mean that Elven Gard lost even under such conditions?"

—It was true that the Eastern Union had been put into a spot in which they had to accept this match. But, if one assumed Sora's interpretation to be correct, it was simply a challenge against the Eastern Union to a game in which *they could cheat all they wanted*.

Just as before, there was no question that they would take away a certain victory—but. To this, Sora only *sneered and answered*:

"Gramps, if you'd known how I managed to communicate with you from the library—if you could really read my thoughts, you wouldn't just be *pretending you knew*. You'd be openly showing surprise."

Looking into Ino's eyes, and, as if tripping him up. Sora spoke with a deeply malicious smile as he played his ultimate trump card.

"Surprise that we're—*not humans of this world*."

—That, in their *old world*, among the countless rumors, there was one about a gamer emerging unbeaten in over 280 games, ascending to urban legend—Ino couldn't see.

He couldn't see that *even cheats and tool assists wouldn't be enough to beat them...*

"......"

Reflexively, Ino tried to dismiss it as a lie. But in no motion or sound of Sora's was there a reaction indicating a lie. If his words were a lie, it would mean that this man could lie without reacting in the slightest. If his words were the truth, it would demonstrate, just as the man said, that he couldn't read minds.

"......!"

In either case—Ino was left with nothing to say. *Yeah, that's what I thought*, Sora seemed to laugh.

"When I came, I bet you thought, 'Here comes a sucker,' just like the old king."

But—.

"—Sorry, but, this time, it's *your turn to suck it*—Werebeast."

Ino could sense no reaction other than conviction from the heartbeat of Immanity's king as he said this, so he merely gulped.

"So."

As Sora stood up, everyone rushed to imitate him.

"That's all. Well, I know you probably don't have the authority to make some craaazy wager like *your entire continental domain* on your own, so why don't you go check with the big guys back home and then let me know when we're playing."

Oh, yeah—he added as if an afterthought:

"This goes without saying, but, for a game betting the Race Piece, *all members of Immanity have a right to watch.* Make sure you get the venue and equipment set up for that? Also, we're going to *take you on as a team of four.* You don't get to say anything about it, so see ya."

Sora, singing this merrily, waved to Izuna, still seated across from him.

"Nice meeting ya, Izzy; next time we're gonna play, yeah?"

"...I don't get this shit, please. But—"

But without a trace of the warmth she had just been showing.

"Sora, and Shiro—you're...trying to pick a fight, please?"

Her eyes were those of one with an investment in staring down an enemy. Of one with a duty to protect something—of an animal poised for battle.

"A fight? Naww. Just a game."

Though Sora said this, still Izuna stared with keen eyes.

"Still makes us *enemies*, please."

Her eyes filling with clear hostility, the little Werebeast girl growled:

"You're goin' down, please."

Yet Sora responded with eyes that in contrast felt friendly.

"Sorry, but *you are going down*, Izuna, without a doubt. Blank doesn't lose."

"...Bye-bye... Izzy, see you later..."

As if chasing the siblings as they playfully and wispily waved and left, Jibril followed, lifting up Steph, covering her mouth as she struggled. Watching the backs of these four as they walked out of the reception chamber, watching the door close as they pressed the elevator button without hesitation, neither Ino Hatsuse and Izuna Hatsuse could say a word...

■■■

"Wh-wh-what have you dooooooooooooooooooooooooooooooooooooooooooooooooooooooooooooooooooooooooooooooooooooooone!!"

Just as they got back to the castle, Steph screamed this, as Sora covered his ears.

"Wh-wh-why did you just do that without saying anything in advance!!"

"If I did, you'd have said no, right?"

At Sora, telling her as he sat on the throne playing a wireless match with Shiro on their DSPs, Steph roared furiously.

"O-of of course I would have! D-do you even understand what you've done?"

"I blocked the enemy's escape by putting the lives of three million Immanities on the line."

—So? Sora seemed to say as he answered blankly. Steph, almost at a loss, somehow managed to squeeze out:

"A-a-and just how do you intend to take responsibility if you lose?"

But at the words that came back…

"Responsibility? What responsibility?"

…Steph finally had nothing to say.

"If we lose, then Immanity is over. What kind of responsibility would there be to take?"

Sora spoke as if he had no interest whatsoever in such things.

"But, come on, Steph—aren't you *excited*?"

No—he was in fact starting to smile, as if he thought it was somehow cool.

"If we lose, then we take the lives of three million Immanities with us and it'll be 'game over.' If we win, we double our territory in one fell swoop, and we grab up all the animal-girls in the Eastern

Union—this has gotta be one of the most exciting games ever. Aren't you pumped?"

"...(*Nod, nod!*)..."

At Sora, smiling innocently, and Shiro, flapping her legs contentedly on his lap, Steph just felt a jolt of something chilly down her spine.

——They were insane. It was not appropriate to describe these siblings by oblique expressions such as "unsound" or "unhinged." Correctly. Truly. In the literal sense—they were *insane*.

"I-is this how you treat human...human life...?"

At this madness, madness beyond mere scorn, Steph felt fear. She wanted to run away, to escape, as she whispered on the verge of tears.

"I've lost all hope I ever had in you...! I thought that, no matter what preposterous antics you got up to, it was all for the sake of the human race, but I was so wrong—!"

Steph denouncing Sora itself was a scene that had been seen many times. But this time, it was clearly different from before; her eyes were full of genuine contempt and disillusionment.

Sora grinned frivolously and answered.

"Cool it, Steph... *It's a game, you know?*"

—With this, Steph's suspicion turned to conviction. To have believed in this man—she had been wrong. This man, no, both of these siblings were just playing. They didn't really care about Immanity or the Eastern Union. *They just thought this whole world was a game—!!*

—*I was wrong to entrust Grandfather's legacy to this craven scoundrel—!* Despair, disillusionment, terror—as Steph was stirred up by countless emotions, by contrast there was Jibril, who as she attended on Sora and Shiro with even deeper respect, said:

"How wise is my master... This is the proof of one fit to rule over us—"

—For the sake of victory, he would even put the lives of the masses on the line. This was not recklessness or abandon, but a *confirmation* of *certain victory*. Steph, in regard to Sora and Shiro, responded

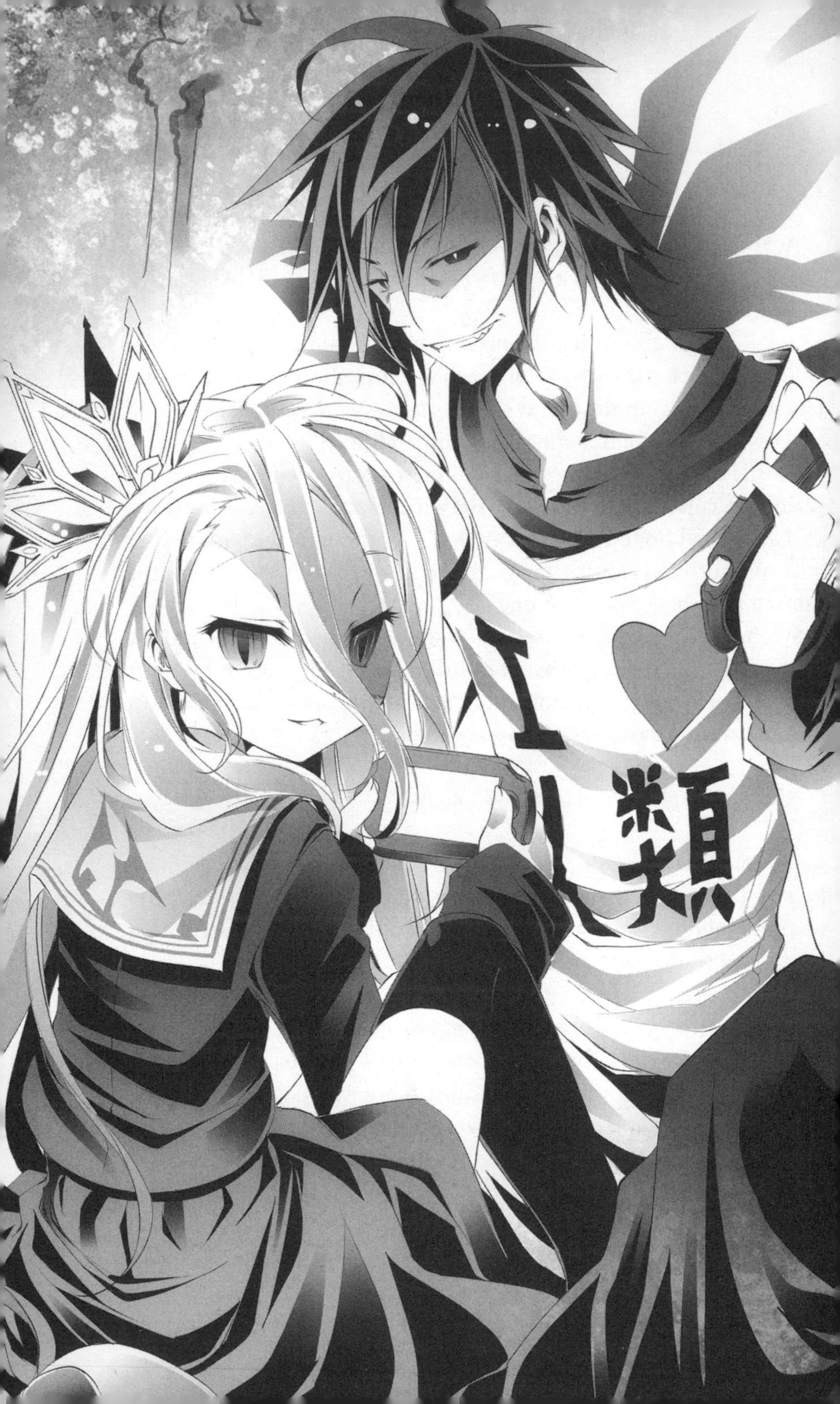
I
類

to the unknown with fear. But, to Jibril, this very same *unknown* pointed the way to adoration, envy, and fascination.

"Wh-what are you talking about! How could he—"
"Then let me ask you a question, little Dora."
Steph flinched under Jibril's uncharacteristically serious gaze.
"You asked how he would take responsibility if he lost, but think about it the other way. If my masters are victorious, then all the Werebeasts in their continental domain will be stripped of their jobs and their rights to their land and assets, left to wander the streets, perhaps even to die. Do you ask that my master take responsibility for *that*? Or would you say *it is their responsibility for losing*?"
"—W-well…that's…"
She had no argument. But, even so—Sora's actions were just too irresponsible. At least…at least the people should have been consulted or something, yes? But Jibril went on.

"Even now that war has been forbidden, killing and being killed still continue in this world."
—A world where force of arms had been forbidden. But, conversely, that was all. It was simple to take, to dominate, to kill by indirect means. This was the nature of the Ten Covenants, and also. Exactly what had happened to Immanity until now.
"Dora, do you propose that Immanity not participate and instead simply perish?"
"W-well…no, but—! Still!"
Still, to say that then they had no responsibility was…it was crazy, insisted Steph.
"This is what being an agent plenipotentiary is about."
Jibril, who herself was part of the agent plenipotentiary of the Flügel, gave Steph an icy glare devoid of feeling, and stated the facts.
"To begin with, reality and games both are about killing each other—what kind of responsibility do you expect?"
—At these too-heavy words from one who had lived through the

bygone Great War, Steph fell silent. But unexpectedly it was Sora who spoke up to contradict.

"Huh? No, no one's gonna die. Didn't I just say it's a *game*?"

"—What?"
"Pardon?"
"Uh?"
"…Mnn…?"
As if something didn't fit. Everyone blanked out. Then Sora spoke, as if he'd finally understood.
"Ohhh… Okay, okay, I get it now; that's how it is."
Sora, had finally identified the unease he'd been feeling all along.
"Yeaaah, I thought this world was weirdly creaky even though everything's decided by games, but, man, you guys—you were really thinking just like those *guys back in our old world*… I didn't see this coming."
"…Ohh…"
Shiro perhaps having wondered about the same thing, nodded looking as if she got it.
"I see, so no one knows how to beat this game—no wonder God got bored and called us."
But, as if he'd had his moment to revel in understanding. He brought his gaze straight back to the game console in his hands and answered vaguely.
"Well, relax. We'll *conquer the world just like we said we would*. All of it, whabam, no two ways about it."
Then, as if remembering something, he continued:
"Oh, yeah, and Steph."
"Ah…wh-what is it?"
"I'll give you a real answer to your question of what happens if we lose."
Without a trace of his clowning from a moment before. Looking into Steph's eyes with a serious gaze, Sora spoke.

* * *

"—There isn't even a one-in-a-million chance we might lose. Didn't I tell you? It's *checkmate*."

These decisive words of Sora—

"Our game with the Eastern Union is *already done*. It's already impossible for them to beat us."

—They went so far over her head, there was in the end no way Steph could believe them.

"Well, to be precise, there is one last missing piece—but we'll have it soon enough.

"Until then, all we have to do is play some games and wait," Sora finished, then went back to the game with his sister.

—The only one who got it was his sister. What was left was a countless set of hints, and two who could not follow those hints to the answer.

Jibril and Steph could only—look at each other.

⏻ FAKE END

…It had been one week since their incursion into the embassy of the Eastern Union and their declaration of hostilities.

The rumor that Sora had bet the Race Piece had started somewhere and spread all at once. Considering that Sora had beaten an Elf spy in the tournament to decide the monarch and then even defeated a Flügel, a notion was growing—"What if Sora himself is a foreign spy?" The nobles who had already had a bone to pick with Sora fanned the flames, and protests broke out. The Elkia Royal Castle was surrounded by crowds, and day after day words of abuse rained down.

—And so, with weary steps, Steph appeared in the throne room and mumbled:
"Sora…I cannot control it any longer…"
The doubts being cast on Sora had spread even to the ministers. There were even some ministers participating in the protests.
"Even the nobles who had been on your side have said that they cannot defend you now… And now the ministers are going on strike, leaving Elkia in a de facto state of anarchy…"

Though Steph must have been just as mistrustful of Sora. She'd apparently done everything to try to keep things steady. As if out of options, she dropped on the floor, reporting.

"Good work, Steph. But everything will be resolved once we finish our game with the Eastern Union."

As usual, as he sat on the throne playing a game with Shiro, Sora praised Steph's efforts, but at the same time gave a wry smile.

"They're saying we're foreign spies? *It's kinda late.* Shoulda thought of that when we beat Elf's spy."

—Indeed. Before Sora, laughing at his people, Steph could not wipe away her mistrust, after all.

"…What are you planning to do? They're even holding a demonstration outside."

"Whatever; let them do what they want."

In this world, it made no difference if they held a demonstration. If they had a problem with Sora's decision—*their only option was to seize the authority of the agent plenipotentiary.*

—But no one had come to challenge them. In other words, that was all the nerve they had.

"…Then, may I ask you what you have been doing in this last week?"

Her question was half ironic and half genuinely seeking an explanation. But the answer that returned was terse.

"Waiting."

That was all.

"…For the Eastern Union to answer that they accept, you mean?"

"Mmm, nah, not really ready for that yet; I want them to wait a little longer."

With this cryptic reply, Sora continued.

"There's one more 'piece' I want to come first—jeez, what's taking so long…"

As Sora vented at *some unknown party,* Jibril came from the side at which she'd been waiting and reacted.

"—Master, this…"

But before Jibril could finish, Sora cut her off with his hand and spoke.

"Oh, you're finally *here*. You ever heard of timeliness?"

—Everyone tracing Sora's line of sight. But at the end of that line was no one. Jibril might have just felt the presence of something. Yet, to the entity invisible to Steph—and *even to Shiro*—Sora talked.

"Yeah, I know why you're here. I'm ready anytime, of course."

—With this, he picked Shiro up from his lap and stood her on the floor. Then he got up himself and looked around.

…Glaring audaciously at Shiro, Steph, Jibril, and that entity visible only to him, Sora, after a long exhalation, said to Shiro:

"Shiro, listen closely."

"…Mnn?"

"I believe in you."

"…I believe in you, too."

While Shiro responded without hesitation, he returned only a smile.

"Shiro, we are *always two in one*."

"Shiro, we are *bound by a promise*."

"Shiro, we are *not the main characters of a boys' manga*."

"Shiro, we are *always victorious before the game starts*."

At Sora's calm spelling out of these statements of obscure meaning. Somehow—

"…Brother…?"

Getting a sickening feeling. Shiro called her brother with unease. Sora, glowing in response, rubbing her head, said:

"—Let's go grab the last piece we need to swallow up the Eastern Union."

And then—facing *that*, he smiled and spoke.

* * *

"—Come, shall we begin the game?"

…—

……—

■■■

The sun slid through the window and her eyelids.

"…Mm…nngh…"

But, her consciousness resisting wakefulness in favor of further dozing, Shiro just turned once to sleep again, faithful to her desire to sleep more. Grasping her brother's arm as usual—but. Her hand, groping around while her eyes remained closed, flailed vainly without grabbing on to what should have been there.

"…Ngh?"

Perhaps—she'd fallen off the bed again. But through her sleep-dimmed head she remembered that she was not sleeping in the bed of the royal bedchamber anymore. Reluctantly, she opened her dazed eyes to look for her brother and grab on to him, but—. The person—who was supposed to always be there—…

——……

The Kingdom of Elkia: the capital, Elkia. In this city, now the last bastion of Immanity after losing territory in one failed bid for dominion after another. In a corridor of the Royal Castle, a girl walked unsteadily. Stephanie Dola. A red-haired, blue-eyed noble girl of the finest breeding, granddaughter of the previous king.

—However, the deep fatigue indicated by the dark circles under her eyes and her heavy steps robbed the young lady of her natural refinement. Clutching playing cards with a creepy smile, wobbling her way to the bedchamber of the king, she gave the impression instead of…a ghost.

"Heh, heh-heh-heh... This is the day you get what's coming to you."

As the newly risen sun came to reap her post-all-nighter consciousness. Stephanie—aka Steph—chuckled restlessly.

"—*Shiro*, you're awake, aren't you?! It's morning!"

Bam, bam. Her hands preoccupied with cards, Steph kicked the door, rudely addressing the queen by her first name. But...Perhaps the door had not been shut properly. For her knock was enough to open it smoothly—

"U-um... Could it be you're awake...?"

—and Steph peered into the royal bedchamber, but. What she saw—

"Brother... Brother, where arrre you... I'm...sorry...it was my fault... I...won't fall out, of bed...anymore...so pleaase come out... eugh..."

—was Shiro, knees in arms, only trembling and crying big tears.

"—H—uh—wh-what's wrong, Shiro?!"

Steph, who'd just a moment ago been snorting about Shiro getting what was coming to her. Was so shocked by the sight that she dropped the cards on the ground and ran to Shiro.

"Wh-what's wrong; are you sick?!"

But, as though she didn't even hear Steph. Shiro just went on crying and muttering:

"Brother...Brother... Come ouut... Don't leave me a...looone..."

Steph, appearing sincerely troubled by her mutterings, said:

"U-um... Whom do you mean by 'Brother'? I-I just have to bring him to you, yes?"

——Then. Steph's words finally made it into Shiro's ears. What was—Steph saying? Shiro only had one *brother*. Shiro took out her phone and opened her contact list—but.

"...No way..."

—That couldn't be. There was only one number registered in Shiro's phone: her brother's. Yet. Why—. Why did her phone say—*0 Contacts*?

* * *

"…That's impossible… No way…no way, no way…"

Seeing the blood drain from skin already white. Steph felt something of no small importance and spoke to Shiro desperately.

"Sh-Shiro, please, are you all right?! Tell me what is wrong!!"

But Shiro seemed no longer to even realize that Steph was there. As she furiously went through her phone's e-mail records, game accounts, addresses, she opened her image folder, opening the subfolders—no.

—There was no trace of her brother.

"…No way… This…can't be…"

In a panic, Shiro checked the date on the phone.

—The twenty-first. Her brother had been playing a game with her on the throne—on the nineteenth. Shiro instantly *went back through her photographic memory*, through all the portable game console, tablet, and phone displays she had seen, and checked that they said *19*. Yes, it had definitely been the nineteenth. But then it should be the twentieth.

—So what had she done *yesterday*?

—…No. She had no memory—whatsoever. The memory of Shiro, able to read books she'd read five years ago backward from memory alone had a complete gap, as if she'd slept through a whole day.

—Her brother was not at her side. He wasn't in her phone's contact list. He didn't appear in e-mails or records or logs or anything.

—Her brother could not be demonstrated to exist *at all*. Having pieced together the situation, Shiro could come up with only *three* possibilities.

Possibility 1: Some unknown force had erased her brother's very existence from this world.

Possibility 2: She had finally lost it.

Possibility 3: She had already lost it—and *she was just now regaining her sanity*.

* * *

But, regardless of which of these possibilities was correct, none, to Shiro, was an answer sufficient to hold the darkness back from overcoming her vision. With a wavering voice, with difficulty, she opened her mouth.

—To say what she hadn't yet said, since she could guess the answer but by no means wanted to hear it. With the last of her hope—she said *his name* to Steph.

"...Ste-ph... Where is Brother... Where is *Sora*...?"

But the answer she then received was, as she'd guessed.

—The answer she'd wanted desperately not to hear.

"...*Sora*? That is someone's name, correct? *Who is that*?"

—Oh.

——Please. Let this be only a *terrible, awful dream*. Let me wake up and find my brother sleeping there as always. Let him just tell me—"Good morning." That was all she wished for as she surrendered herself to the darkness that overcame her.

—Shiro let go of her consciousness.

TO BE CONTINUED

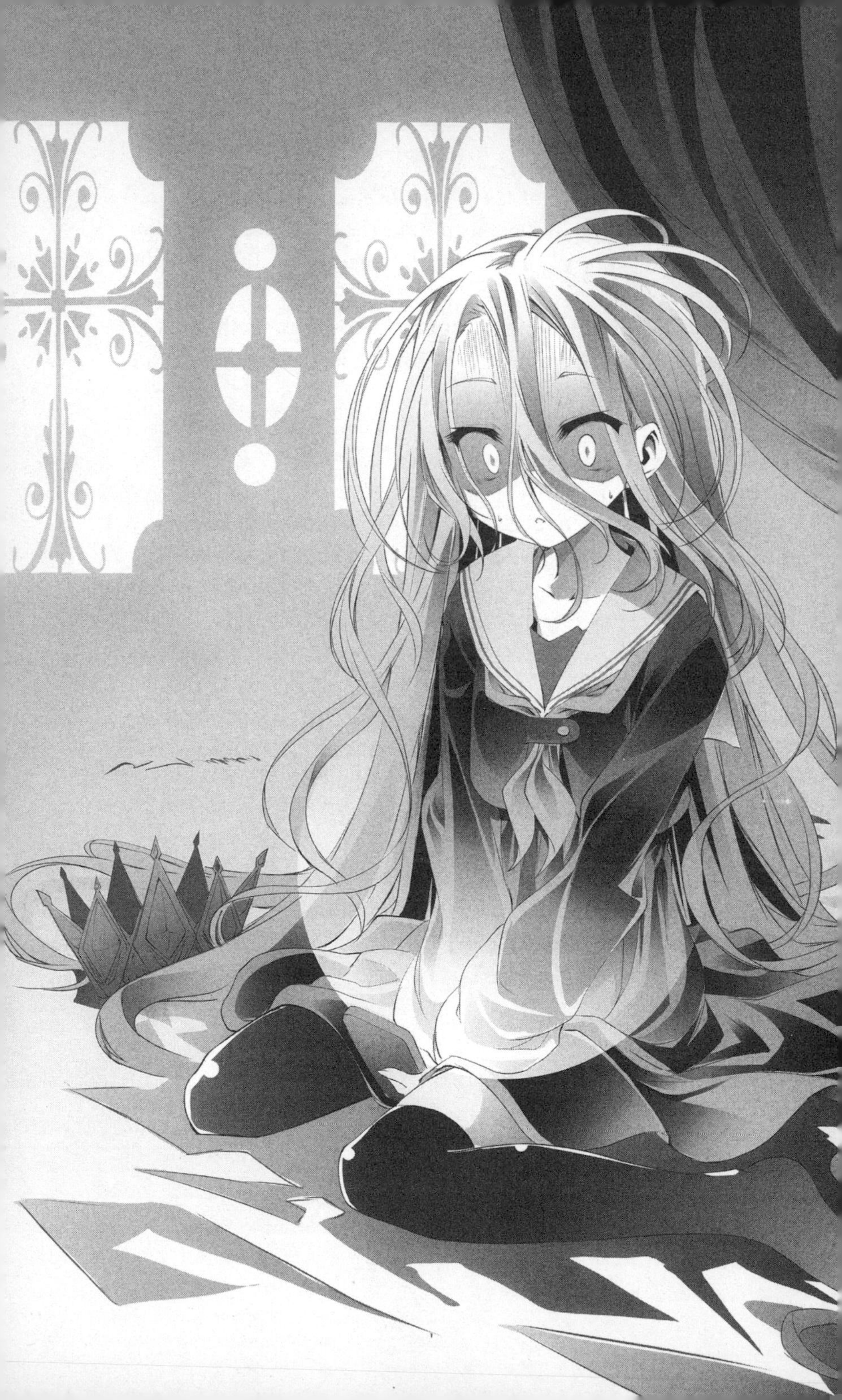

⏻ AFTERWORD

Hello, nice to see you again, it's the author and illustrator, Yuu Kamiya.

—I-it looks as if somehow we've made it all right to the second volume being published, and for that I could not be more grateful. I mean, I have already had some experience with my manga and books with my illustrations going on store shelves. But, you know, I'm still totally a novice when it comes to writing light novels. I wrote it all and sent it in, and then much later I hear now it's going on store shelves and I finally realize it's for real. And then my stomach starts hurting from the stress, so before I know it I've fled to *Skyr*m* and I'm casting mad buffs on my weapons and venturing into ruins and collecting books and enjoying my alternate life in a literal other world with my hobby of gaming! And then my editor calls me and pulls me back to reality and it's already been released! Thanks to this, I have succeeded spectacularly in bypassing the pressure!

"Ahem… Perhaps you could say that you were escaping from reality into your second manuscript; you really don't have to tell the truth about this."

Oh! If it isn't Editor S! Editor S for Sadist, who told me,
Wait, did I not tell you about the deadline for the promo materials?
or something like that, all of a sudden before the deadline? Well,
by the second volume, you've become a regular tradition, haven't
you! Yeah, I was just wondering what the hell you were going to do
to—

"Well, you see? Considering you *hadn't finished the manuscript*, I
thought it might be too much to order the art at this point."
...I'm sorry.

"Actually, Mr. Kamiya, in the first place, could you please not
finish a whole manuscript for a second volume and then say you're
scrapping it?"
...I'm sorry...

"Also, I understand that going back and forth between Brazil
and Japan causes you to philosophize seriously about borders and
trade, but if you could please refrain from then saying, 'Ah, whatever,' and blithely restructuring the manuscript you supposedly had
finished by then..."
...I'm sorry I was born...

Uh, uhh, let's start over! Okay, the content of this volume was
actually supposed to be in the first volume originally. The content
of the first volume was supposed to be chapter 1, this volume was
chapter 2, and the third volume was chapter 3—see. I do in fact have
my early outline where I wrote some mysterious babbling like that,
right here!

"...Were you planning to submit a nine-hundred-page book?"
W-well... I guess I didn't know how much text goes in one novel
volume, or the distribution... A-a-anyway, with the next volume,
Sora and Shiro will collect the "minimum hand" they need to
conquer the world. Since, as of this volume, they've already got a
"checkmate," as Sora says. Those of you who are reading the afterword first, as well as those of you who have already read the volume,
why not try to anticipate Sora's thoughts—Wait, if you get it right,
I think I'll be depressed, so maybe don't...please...uh.

…Well. There's still more space in this volume, so welcome to Outtake Zone. Here, they're playing Materialization Shiritori, so.

"…Whatever. Then I'll pick something safe—'meat.'"

And Sora's word was materialized.

…But…uh?

"Excuse me—why does *meat* make a *buxom blond girl* appear?!"

In contrast to the sparkling smile of Jibril, the cold eyes of Shiro.

"Brother, your image…"

"O-ohh…sorry, it looks like it got influenced by the image in my head?"

—Yeah, there was a passage like that…

"Ehh… That seems somewhat inappropriate…"

Yes, I know. If you could materialize fictional entities, then you could say "chrono-quake bomb" and then the universe would be in rather bad shape, so I tearfully scrapped it. Oh, but that ends in "n" (against normal *shiritori* rules).*

"No, that's not exactly what I meant."

And if that means Sora thinks of this every time he eats meat— well, I guess that's okay?

"I wouldn't say that? (*sunny smile*)"

By the way, I wrote over half of this volume in Brazil. In connection with the disease I mentioned in the previous volume, it was decided that I'd be going back to Brazil seriously, for a few years. So, to judge whether I could keep writing as I have been while living in Brazil, how much my life would be impacted, etc., I tried staying at a month-to-month apartment instead of with my relatives.

—Conclusion: No. Cannot work in Brazil.

"…Eh? Isn't it your native country? Is there some problem—"

Yes, there is! Every time there's a soccer match, *the whole town shakes*, you know?!

"……You're not talking about an earthquake?"

There are cheers and fireworks; every time there's a goal, everyone in the building goes crazy!

"...Well, that does sound like something you'd imagine happening in Brazil..."

I mean, I like soccer, too, but! To have that ruckus going on day after day, night after night, I can't concentrate, I can't sleep, and, most important!! Pops! I'm telling you I've got a deadline; stop grabbing my hand every time they make a goal and dancing a—

"By the way, Mr. Kamiya, it's about time for those pages."

...What? No, uh, the illustrations still aren't—

"I'm sure you can make it work somehow!"

Here, everything is decided by games...

In a world where even lives and borders are decided by games, Immanity has been cornered by other races with magic and supernatural powers down to their last city.

Now their fate lies in the hands of just two gamers!!

HEY, STEPH WHERE DO BABIE COME FROM?

Reps of Immanity shut-in, loser, game veg bro Sora and sis Shiro

SO LONG, IMMANITY ...

Stephanie Dola

No No Game Life

Flügel—Jibril

The weakest race—

COULD YOU MEAN A FRAIL HUMAN...

...CHAL-LENGES ME?

OU'RE HE NE O'S MB.

IF YOU THINK BEING TOUGH AND LONG-LIVED IS POWER...

NI CGRIND

—takes on Flügel, Werebeast—

THEY ARE COMING TO MY DOOR-STEP...

...AND YOU GUYS CAN'T STOP IT.

OTG—Tet

—and even God?

EDITOR, IT JUST OCCURRED TO ME...

HOW CAN YOU WIN AGAINST MAGICAL CHEATERS?

DONYORI CGLOOMD

Can you follow the twists that even the author can't predict—?!

H-h-how does th-th-that look?

"…? Why are you acting so tense?"

Uh, uhh, well, I just couldn't make enough time, so…you see. The one who drew this——**isn't me**.

"——Pardon?"

U-um, I just made the storyboard, and the one who actually drew it was, uh…my…wife?

"………"

I-I know you're going to say I'm too free and easy! B-b-but you were the one who tacitly pressured me into putting manga in the afterword, right? And my wife is in the same industry, you know… she's an illustrator by the name of Mashiro Hiiragi. S-so can you please somehow overlook—hey. Editor, why are you staring at my manuscript like that?

"Mr. Kamiya, why don't we get started on the comic version. As a husband-wife joint project. ♥"

You monster!!

* * *

I-I mean, to begin with, didn't I say I was taking a break from manga because of my health?!

"Well, sure, it might be difficult for you by yourself, but—"

No, look, I'm just going to lay this out here, but I started writing these light novels because I thought it would be easier on my health than manga, but now that I look at it there's the illustrations and revisions and in the end it's just—

"But you come through in the end, don't you? (*sunny smile*)"

Oh, it's time for my flight, I'd better run away—I mean, I have to run!

"Oh, Mr. Kamiya, just where are you intending to go?"

But was blocked in front!

U-umm, everyone who's read this far, please pick up the next volume, too! I hope you've found something to enjoy in this second volume, accelerated by rush! So, I hope to meet you again, and, with that, I run!

"Mr. Kamiyaaa, we know where you live and your telephone number and face, hee-hee-hee-hee-hee…"

TWO IN ONE

PROMISE

MAIN CHARACTER OF A BOYS' MANGA

BEFORE THE GAME STARTS...

MEMORIES LOST
WORDS LEFT

THE FINAL PIECE TO TRANSFORM CERTAIN
DEFEAT INTO CERTAIN VICTORY...?

IN NO GAME NO LIFE, VOLUME 3,
SWALLOWING UP THE THIRD-
LARGEST NATION IN THE WORLD!!
OUT PRETTY SOON...PROBABLY!

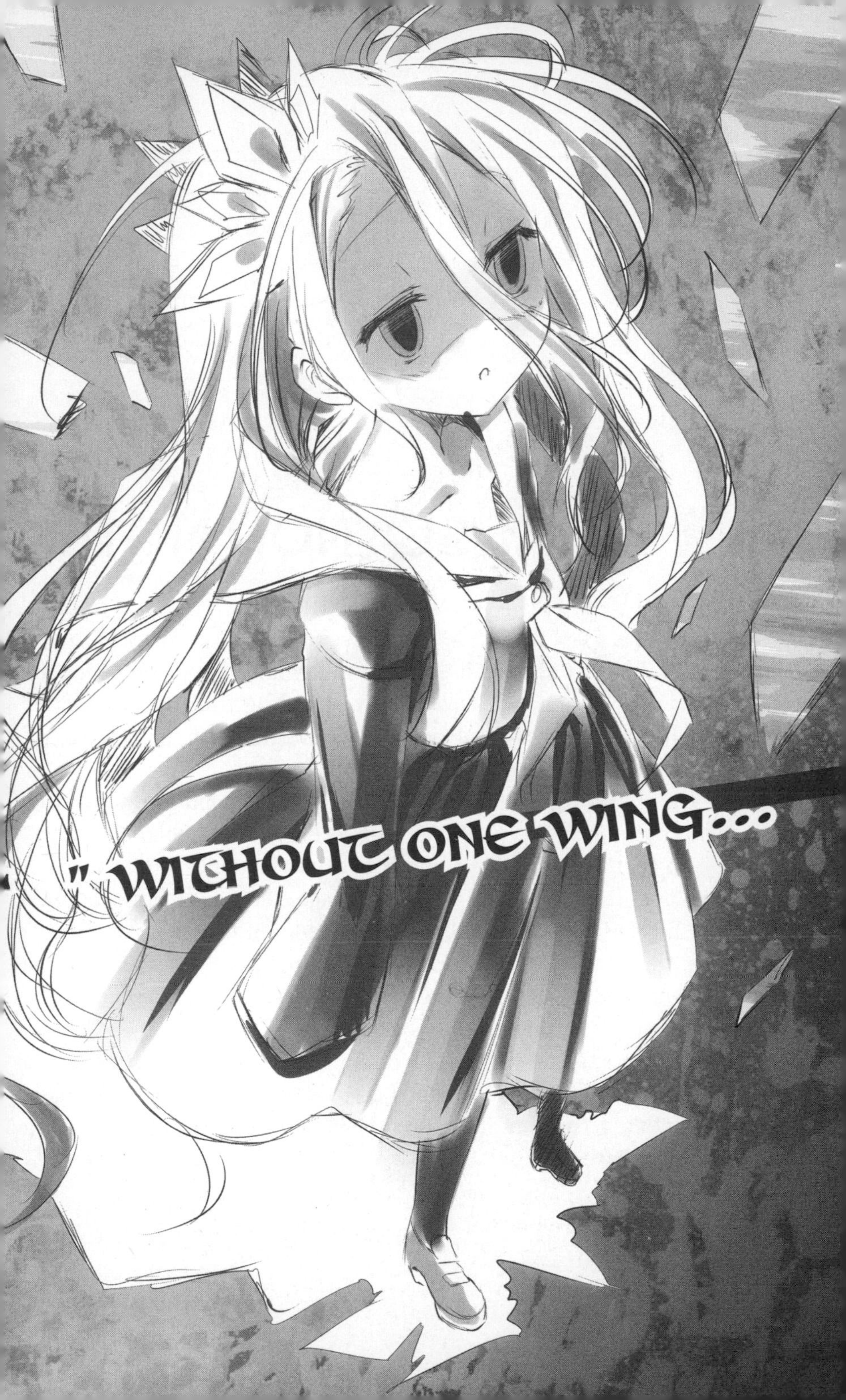
"WITHOUT ONE WING..."

TRANSLATION NOTES

Shiritori is a Japanese word game in which players take turns saying words. Each word must begin with the syllable (*kana*) on which the previous word ended. Playing a word ending with the syllable "n" results in a loss, since no Japanese word begins with the syllabic "n," as the author references in his afterword.

The *shiritori* game that played out in the second chapter of this volume of *No Game No Life* represented a particular challenge, given that it involved the rather constricting rules cited above. In the first printing of the English-language edition, the game retained the Japanese words that each side played, but for the second printing, the editorial team undertook the challenge of translating the action, modifying the rules to match first and last letters of the words employed, rather than syllables.

For the readers' reference, romanizations of the original terms utilized for each turn are listed below, along with the literal translation of the term from the original Japanese edition. Their matching syllables have been italicized.

- Suiba*ku* [H-bomb]
- *Kú* Li An*se*

- *Seirei Kairou* [Spirit Corridors]
- *U·ma* [Horse]
- *Ma*ko* [P*ssy]

- *Break in game play*

- *Biichi* [Beach]
- *Chikubi* [Nipples]
- *Bikini* [Bikini]
- *Nimotsu* [Baggage]
- *Tsumuji* [Dust Devil]
- *Joseifuku* [Ladies' Wear]
- *Kuroobaa* [Clover]

- *Break in game play*

- *Mantoru* [Mantle]
- *Ruiaaga*
- *Gaikaku* [Outer Core]
- *Kurokku* [Clock]
- *Kuriichaa* [Creature]
- *Akari* [Lamp]
- *Risosufia* [Lithosphere]
- *A·sa* [Morning]
- *Sanso* [Oxygen]
- *Sonata* [Sonata]
- *Tane*-ue [Seed Planter]
- *E·a* [Air]
- *Atomosufea* [Atmosphere]
- *Anjaku* [Feebleminded]
- *Kuuronryoku* [Coulomb Force]

Author Afterword *Shiritori*
- Niku [Meat]
- Jukkushin-Bakudan [Chrono-Quake Bomb]

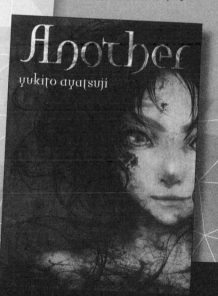

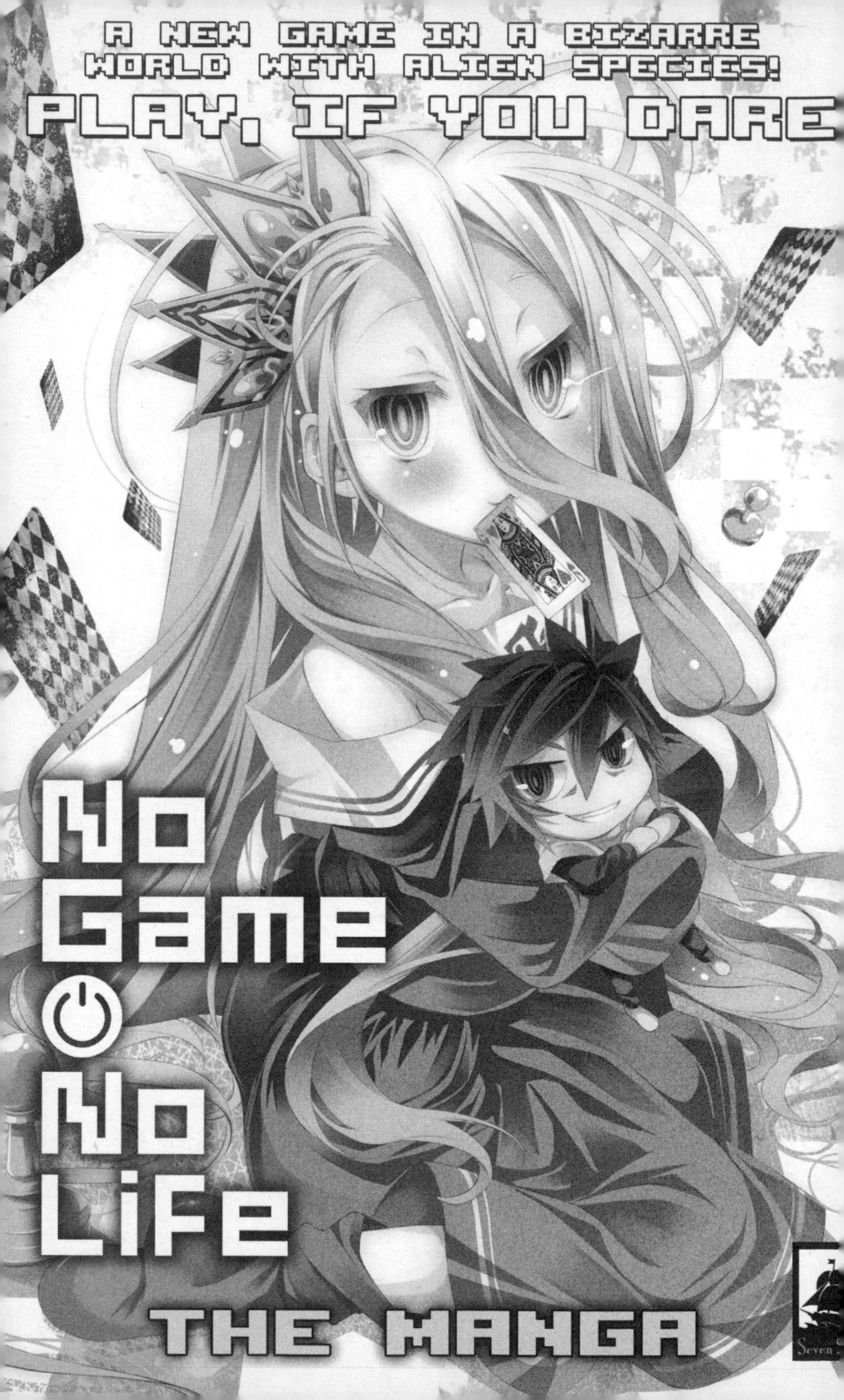
A NEW GAME IN A BIZARRE WORLD WITH ALIEN SPECIES!
PLAY, IF YOU DARE
No Game No Life
THE MANGA